F

303385844 6

D1784101

Louisa Heaton lives on Hayling Island, Hampshire, with her husband, four children and a small zoo. She has worked in various roles in the health industry—most recently four years as a Community First Responder, answering 999 calls. When not writing Louisa enjoys other creative pursuits, including reading, quilting and patchwork— usually instead of the things she *ought* to be doing!

Also by Louisa Heaton

The Icelandic Doc's Baby Surprise
Risking Her Heart on the Trauma Doc
A Baby to Rescue Their Hearts
Twins for the Neurosurgeon
A GP Worth Staying For
Their Marriage Meant To Be
Their Marriage Worth Fighting For
A Date with Her Best Friend
Miracle Twins for the Midwife

Discover more at millsandboon.co.uk.

THE BROODING DOC AND THE SINGLE MUM

LOUISA HEATON

MILLS & BOON

First published in Great Britain 2023
by Mills & Boon, an imprint of HarperCollins*Publishers* Ltd,
1 London Bridge Street, London, SE1 9GF

www.harpercollins.co.uk

HarperCollins*Publishers*
Macken House, 39/40 Mayor Street Upper,
Dublin 1, D01 C9W8, Ireland

Large Print edition 2023

ISBN: 978-0-263-30759-7

11/23

To Sheila H and Sheila C

CHAPTER ONE

Greenbeck Village Welcomes
Careful Drivers
Twinned with Vebnice, Croatia

Dr Stacey Emery smiled as she drove past
the sign, glancing briefly into the rear-view
mirror. Her son, Jack, was looking out of the
window at a field filled with sheep and new
lambs. 'We're here!' she beamed, hoping to
see him smile and fill him with some excite-
ment about their move. But he didn't even
meet her eyes.

She did worry about him. This move to
Greenbeck was meant to be the answer to
all their problems and worries. Their fresh
start. Their reset button. All her hopes and
dreams were pinned on Greenbeck working
its extraordinary magic and bringing back
the fun-filled, happy boy she'd used to know.

Greenbeck had been her childhood home

and she had many wonderful memories here. She couldn't remember a time when she hadn't been happy. It had always seemed to be summer. Sunshine…warmth on her face. Flowers. Playing with her friends. Feeding the ducks at the duckpond. Watching the canal barges drift beneath the Wishing Bridge. Calling to the people on the boats and waving.

She'd grown up on Blossom Lane, where the only traffic she'd had to be careful of was the horses being led out through the gate of High Field Farm. Whenever they'd come she'd run inside to tell her grandad to bring his shovel, because said horses had left some helpful, steaming piles of manure on the road he could acquire for his rose bushes and vegetable patch.

She'd picked blackberries and gooseberries from wild bushes. Scrumped apples from Merryman's Orchard. Swung on a swing above the brook. Paddled barefoot in the water, looking for sticklebacks with a bright neon-yellow net on the end of a bamboo cane. There'd been the fun of the village fete. Skipping to school. Sports days with egg and spoon races...

Apart from when she'd lost her parents, Stacey couldn't remember a time here when she hadn't smiled. And she needed that for Jack.

She couldn't remember the last time he'd truly been happy. Truly laughed. Truly enjoyed being a little boy.

She needed, desperately, for Greenbeck and her grandparents to work their magic all over again.

But she'd been away for so long. She hoped and prayed that the village had somehow ignored the passage of time and was still exactly as she remembered it.

The road after the sign would lead her down into the valley where Greenbeck nestled. She drove past the ancient ruins of Castle Merrick, a place she'd often looked up at and dreamed was filled with the ghosts of lords and ladies from centuries past. It was now a heritage site and she could see tourists gathering. Its one last turret stood formidably high, defiant against the years, casting a shadow over the road that suddenly began to twist and turn as it took her through the woods.

The green canopy of trees high above flickered with the snippets of sun breaking through, dotting the road and her windscreen with a dazzling array of strobing light. Then the car broke free from the woods and opened up into bordering fields, where she saw more sheep. Cows… Horses… And was that an alpaca?

A road sign declared that the upper speed limit for driving through Greenbeck was twenty miles per hour, so she slowed down, glad of the chance to look around and re-familiarise herself with a place that she hadn't seen for a long time.

The few visits she'd managed had been way too short. Weekends here and there. Once to introduce her grandparents to her now ex-husband Jerry. Another after Jack had first been born. Her grandparents would have loved to keep their great-grandson in their lives, but it hadn't been possible. Her job had been in Scotland. She'd done what she could…maintaining video calls once a month. But being a single mother didn't often leave her with much time on her hands and so they'd not visited in person as often she would have liked.

Her grandparents, Genevieve and William Clancy, were so proud of her, though. For doing well at school, despite the trauma of losing both her parents in a tragic accident so early on in life. They'd supported her and cheered her on when she'd applied to study medicine at university, waving her off as she'd driven her ancient car away from Greenbeck to travel all the way to Edinburgh.

They'd managed to come up for her graduation ceremony, which had been nice, and had listened to her on the phone each week as she'd described to them what it was like on her hospital placements and then her GP training. And then how it had felt to fall in love.

They'd taken the news in a non-judgemental, wonderful way when she'd told them she'd eloped to Gretna Green to marry a GP she'd met and not invited anyone to the wedding. They'd listened in the same way when her marriage had crumbled after she fell pregnant with Jack…

So much had passed since she'd been away.

So much heartache. So much pain. And not once had they admonished her. Their love for her was eternal and something that could never be broken, it seemed.

Which was what they both needed. Her grandparents knew of Jack's troubles. Knew of Stacey's despair. And when they'd told her, *'Come home. There's a place for Jack at Greenbeck Juniors. We've already checked...'* she had known in her heart it was the right thing to do. It was time to come back home and be healed, despite the memories that impeded the thought of doing so. She'd lost her parents here.

The road took her through the heart of Greenbeck, past the village green, where small families stood by the pond, feeding the ducks and a pair of resident swans. She smiled, remembering the many hours she'd spent doing exactly the same thing.

'Look at all the ducks, Jack!'

He made a non-committal sound in his throat and tightened his grip on his teddy bear, Grover, the stuffed toy he'd become attached to since he was a baby. Grover was a little bedraggled now. Stacey had lost count of the amount of times she'd stitched him up, repairing his paws and ears, because Jack never let him go when he was at home.

Stacey noticed a new building next to the church. Single-storey. Built in the same grey stone that most of the buildings here were constructed with, but with a large, modern glass frontage. *Greenbeck Village Surgery.*

So that's where I'll be working...

When Stacey had been a little girl the doctor had operated out of his own house. Dr Pickwick had been a dour-faced old man. A bit gruff, with steel-rimmed spectacles. But every time her grandma had taken her to see him, either because of illness or for an inoculation, Dr Pickwick had opened up his desk drawer and let her choose from a box of sweeties or lollipops if she'd been a good patient. And sometimes when she'd sat in the waiting room, ready to be seen—actually the front parlour of his home—Stacey had been able to smell whatever Mrs Pickwick was baking.

For a long time she'd associated going to the doctor's with the delicious aroma of apple pie. One of Mrs Pickwick's favourites... But that was for later. And even though she was also keen to call in on her grandparents, whom she hadn't seen in person for a few years, she was very much aware that she'd been driving for hours and what she wanted most was something to eat and drink and maybe to take a shower, so that she could see them when she was feeling refreshed.

There was a parking space over by The Buttered Bun Café and she slid into it, pulling on the handbrake. 'Here we are! Let's grab a quick bite to eat. I don't know about you, but I'm starved.'

She helped Jack clamber from his seat and then she held his hand as they entered The Buttered Bun. Above their heads a bell rang to announce their entrance and, spotting a seat by the window, she parked Jack and gave him one of the complementary colouring sheets and pots of crayons whilst she went to give their order.

There were plenty of delicious-looking treats on display. Sausage rolls, pies, sandwiches, cake slices, cream cakes, gingerbread men… She ordered two hot sausage rolls, one hot chocolate and a pot of tea for herself, paid, then went to sit down. Jack was busy studiously colouring in a dragon in bright purple crayon.

'Wow, that looks amazing,' she said.

'Thanks.'

It was only one word, but it was the most she'd had out of him in hours. It warmed her heart. Made her feel hopeful. She sat and watched him for a few minutes, noting the way his eyebrows were arched in concentration, the way he worried at his bottom lip. Then the waitress, a pretty young woman with red hair almost the same shade as Stacey's, brought over their order.

'Hey, great dragon!' she said.

Stacey saw her name tag: Jade. She smiled, then walked away, went behind her counter, busying herself with making coffee for an elderly gentleman who had come in after Stacey. Who *was* that? He looked familiar. But it had been so long her mind struggled for names from the past.

The sausage roll was perfect. Buttery, crisp pastry with warm, spiced meat inside.

She needed a napkin afterwards to wipe her fingers.

Jack ate most of his, and was just finishing his hot chocolate when the bell sounded above the door again and in rushed the most handsome man Stacey had ever seen in her entire life.

She tried not to stare. But it was hard not to at a man like that!

Already her heart rate had increased, and she sucked in a breath to try and steady it, pretending to take a renewed interest in Jack's colouring, in the hope that he wouldn't notice her.

She'd fallen for a handsome man before and he'd been nothing but trouble. Men like that got noticed everywhere they went. By other women. Other men. They got hit on. Flirted with. And that was often an irresistible thing. It certainly had been to Jerry, her ex-husband. Meaning Stacey had been burned by love. Left as a single mother. And Jack was fatherless. His father wasn't dead. Just absent. Being burdened with a child was not something Jerry had ever wanted.

Why didn't I see it?

So Stacey would quite happily stay away from men who turned heads wherever they went.

She noticed the waitress—Jade—had perked up considerably at the man's entrance. She was beaming a smile at him, eyes gleaming, chest thrust out, fluttering her eyelashes.

'Hi. Can I help you?'

'I've pre-ordered six of your finest white chocolate chip cookies.'

Stacey couldn't help but notice that he was a fine figure of a man. Flat stomach. A hint of muscle beneath his shirtsleeves. Nicely shaped thighs and butt in tailored trousers. He didn't look the sort to gorge on chocolate chip cookies. He looked like an avocado on toast kind of man. A man who knew exactly how much protein he consumed each day. Who could bench-press a considerable weight. Who she would no doubt see jogging around the village most days, looking all hot and sweaty and delicious...

He turned. Glanced her way.

Immediately she turned to Jack, leaning over the table to grab a crayon and help her son complete his picture. Stacey concentrated

hard, until she heard the man finish his trans-
action and the ring of the bell behind her as
he left.

She let out a breath and Jack looked up.

'What is it?'

'Oh. Nothing…'

She glanced at the waitress, who was twirl-
ing her necklace in her fingers as she looked
longingly out through the café's front window, clearly tracking the man's progress.

Stacey shook her head slightly, feeling that
she could easily give some wise, womanly
advice to Jade about watching out for men
like that. But she had enough on her plate
and it was time to go.

'Finished?' she asked Jack.

He nodded.

'Good.' Stacey gathered their things, then
thanked Jade. 'Actually, could you help me?'
she added. 'I'm looking for Blacksmith's Cottage, Honeysuckle Lane. Could you direct
me? I'm not familiar with that road.'

Stacey had assumed it was a new road, built
in the intervening years since she'd been here
last.

Jade looked at her curiously. 'Sure. You

turn right, then head to the end of the High Street. First left, then second right. It's on the edge of the new development site there.'

Where the old blacksmith used to be, Stacey thought. On the edge of the village. Made sense, considering the name of the cottage. 'Thanks,' she said.

'Welcome to Greenbeck.' Jade smiled.

'Thanks,' she said again.

They headed back out to the car. Stacey was keen to get settled in. Offload their belongings. It was a shame they couldn't stay with her grandparents, but there simply wasn't room for both her and Jack. Jack was a growing boy. Her grandparents had offered, but no, it wouldn't have been right. Jack needed his own space, and it would have been unfair to him for them both to squeeze into her old childhood bedroom. Her gran and grandad were getting on in years, too, and it would have been unreasonable to expect them to cope with a noisy young boy—much though she knew they would love having Jack in their lives.

'Come on, Jack. Let's find home.'

* * *

Dr Daniel Prior stood by the mantelpiece, staring at the picture of his wife Penny and his son Mason. It was something he did a lot. Often when he felt alone, or when he had a decision to make in life. As if staring at the image would somehow tell him what to do.

In the picture, Penny and Mason had just released lanterns into the night sky during a holiday in Oahu, Hawaii. Like them, he had stood and watched the lanterns float upwards with hundreds of others, during the lantern festival, and he'd pulled out his mobile to take pictures. The first picture had been of the sky, lit by the multitude of lanterns, and the second picture—the one he was looking at now—was Penny standing behind Mason, her hands on his shoulders, as they'd both turned to look at him, smiling—no, *beaming* in delight.

It had perfectly captured their delight and joy, and in that moment he had loved them both so much he'd thought to himself, *Even if I never get another day it doesn't matter, because right now is perfect.*

'But I was wrong,' he said sadly to the

empty room. 'I'd give anything for another day with you two.'

His wife and son smiled back at him, unaware that their lives would both be cruelly cut short just one day later. The guilt of that thought tortured him even now.

Daniel rubbed at his hip. It still ached. Two years since the accident. If he'd lived, Mason would be six now—in junior school. Penny would be thirty. She'd always had such big plans for her thirtieth birthday party...

Sighing, he turned from the mantelpiece and went to the kitchen to pick up the bag of chocolate chip cookies he'd collected earlier from The Buttered Bun. It wasn't much. Just a little housewarming gift for the new doctor. Or rather an annexe-warming gift.

When the senior partner, Dr Zach Fletcher, had told Daniel he'd hired someone new for their expanding practice he'd offered to put them up until they could find somewhere more permanent. His annexe was empty—it might as well be put to use. The rent would be nice, too. But most of all he knew how hard it was to find a place to buy in Greenbeck.

Since its arrival on the list of the UK's top

ten best villages to live in, places to rent and buy here had become extortionate in price. Not many people left the village, and properties tended to stay within families. An incoming GP would struggle to find a place, so Daniel had kindly offered his annexe as part of the job, for as long as the new doctor needed it.

Zach had told him the new GP, the Clancys' grand-daughter, had lots of experience in her old practice. Apparently, she'd been instrumental in putting together a variety of support groups for her patients: a diabetes support group. A 'Knit and Natter' group for some of her more elderly patients. A 'Men's Shed' for widowers to get together and make new friends. A volunteer support group, and even a group for anxiety sufferers, who apparently took it in turns to meet at each other's houses.

It certainly sounded as if she was a proactive person, and he was looking forward to meeting her. But even though she'd be in his annexe, and they would be colleagues, he hoped that she would respect his boundaries. Colleagues, friends and neighbours they might be, but he wouldn't want them popping in every five minutes. Daniel liked his solitude now that he'd got used to it, and when he went home for the day he treasured his alonetime. It allowed him to recharge his batteries and let go of the stresses of the day.

His doorbell rang and he knew it would be her. She was early. He hadn't had time to leave the cookies in the annexe yet, with the welcome note he'd been going to write.

Oh, well.

He put the cookies down and went to answer his front door. He pulled it open and stood there for a minute, absolutely stupefied at the sight of the young redheaded woman before him, her hands resting on the shoulders of a child who was clearly her son. He was the spitting image of his mother. Redhaired. Freckled. Pale, creamy skin.

There'd beenphotographs on the Clancys' hearth, but he'd never looked at them up close.

'Yes?'

He couldn't help but notice her green eyes. The soft, gentle waves of the long red hair hanging below her shoulders. She was pretty…

No. She's beautiful.

'I'm Dr Stacey Emery. And this is my son, Jack.'

She was looking at him with uncertainty.

Daniel looked down at the boy, who was looking up at him with curiosity.

'Erm…' His brain scrambled madly for something sensible and welcoming to say, but all he could feel was fear and apprehension. Was he ready for this? A young boy? A child who could be the age Mason would be now?

I'll just keep my distance.

'I…er…wasn't expecting you this early. You made good time?'

'Not bad.'

'You must be tired. Let me grab the keys and I'll show you around.'

He grabbed the annexe keys off the hook, and the bag of cookies, and closed his front door behind him, intending to show her the annexe quickly and then leave her to it.

This was the woman that he'd spotted in the café! It had been a quick glance, but enough for him to hope that she wasn't the person he was waiting for. He'd thought for a second that she was someone who looked a bit like Stacey Emery, but hoped it wasn't.

He led the way around the side of his cottage to the annexe that he'd had built at the bottom of his garden. Originally he'd built it as a project in his spare time, intending to use it as a place for his parents to move into. But his mum and dad had begun to require nursing care as they'd got older, and they'd recently moved into a facility in Guildford instead, leaving the new annexe free.

He'd contemplated making it into some kind of studio. He'd had grand plans for making videos about what it was like to be a GP... maybe doing a podcast? Interviewing people with interesting medical stories and posting them online? But all that required that he be quite the extrovert, and he wasn't ready just yet. Renting out the annexe had seemed like a good substitution.

He unlocked the door and pushed it open, stepping back so Dr Emery and her son could go in first.

She gave him a slight smile as she passed, and he couldn't help but inhale the scent of her perfume. Floral. Light. Not overpowering in any way. The kind of scent that made you want to close your eyes and savour it for as long as you could.

But of course he wasn't going to do that, so he just waited a moment or two for them to be in the heart of the living space and then followed them in.

'This is the living area. Kitchen's through there. It's got everything you should need. Dishwasher, cooker, microwave. Cookies.'

He awkwardly placed the brown paper bag on her counter. Not wanting to draw too much focus to the gesture. Hoping she'd let it pass and just accept it as a run-of-the-mill housewarming gift.

'There's a separate utility room out the back. Down there are the two bedrooms and a bathroom, complete with shower.'

He wanted to hand over the keys and get out of there, even if it seemed rude. He was still scrabbling to accept that this was the Clancys' granddaughter, incredibly beautiful, and that she had a son the same age Mason would be, had he not died...

He let out a breath as she turned this way and that, perusing everything. 'You can make any changes you want in regard to furniture,' he said. 'But I'd appreciate it if you could store anything original in the attic space.'

'It all looks wonderful. And bringing the cookies was thoughtful. Thank you.' She smiled, then knelt down to face her son. 'Jack? Want to go choose a bedroom?'

The little boy nodded and sped off down the corridor, clutching a manky-looking teddy bear that had clearly seen better days. It needed to go in the washing machine, but Daniel wasn't sure it would be in one piece after a wash.

The annexe had two double rooms. Both the same size. He'd kept decorations quite minimal, thinking of his parents. White walls. Lots of stained wood. Lots of greenery. He imagined it would all seem a little too grown-up for a young boy.

'If he wants to put up posters and things, that's fine.'

'That's great. I appreciate you letting us stay here for a while. Hopefully it won't be for too long.' She smiled again, lighting up her green eyes.

He nodded. 'You're the Clancys' grand-daughter?'

She seemed surprised that he knew this. 'Yes. You know them?'

'Kind of.'

He couldn't say any more. His mouth didn't seem connected to his brain right now.

He couldn't think of anything else to say to her, so reached out a hand to pass her the keys.

'Here you go. Do you need help with your bags, or…?'

Please don't need help with your bags.

'We'll be fine. Just a couple of cases in the car.'

'Right. Well, I'll leave you to it, then.'

He turned and walked out of the annexe, breathing a huge sigh of relief once he was back in the fresh air.

What a complication! He'd fervently hoped Dr Emery would keep her distance and re-spect his boundaries before she got here, but now he knew that he would have to keep her at arm's length as much as possible. Be-cause, as much as he'd loved his wife and vowed never to look at another woman ever again, he'd felt an instant *something* when he'd opened the door to Dr Emery.

In his experience that *something...*that *spark...*always led to something more, and he wasn't ready for it.

Dr Emery and her young son Jack were a threat. A danger.

And he knew he had to protect himself at all costs.

Oh, no.

That had been her first thought when Dr Prior had opened the door, and the second one that had come tumbling right after it was, *Don't let anything show on your face.*

Dr Prior—the man she was renting her home from, living next-door to, becoming his tenant—was exactly the same man she'd seen rush into The Buttered Bun to collect a bag of cookies. That stunner of a man who now, up close, she could see was even more handsome than she'd realised whilst at the café. Dark-haired, with a well-groomed beard, choco-latey brown eyes, a jawline that was square and proud. And since he'd been in the café he'd removed his tie and opened the neck of his shirt. She'd been able to see the slight hint of a hairy chest upon well-developed muscle.

Her mouth had instantly dried, even as her heart rate had rocketed. Thank God for Jack, who'd stood in front of her like a human shield.

For a brief moment she'd hoped it was a mistake. He'd certainly looked confused by her arrival, as if he'd not been expecting her, and she'd hoped that maybe she'd stopped at the wrong cottage and the address she really needed was next door, or something. But no. She wasn't in the wrong place and this man was going to be her landlord and her new colleague...

Oh, dear God, he's going to be hard not to look at.

That was the problem with beautiful things. You looked at them. Admired them. And admiration turned to wanting, and wanting led to...

It's best I don't think about what that leads to. Dr Prior is off-limits. I'm off-limits.

Her grandparents had said that her new landlord was a nice man. A very good doctor whom they'd known for a few years. So she'd expected someone *older.*

But the annexe was perfect for her and Jack, and Jack looked keen to explore.

Now Dr Prior had handed her the keys and left she was able to take in its features better—without the distraction of an Adonis at her side. It had a large living area, with soft leather sofas, a low coffee table, and bookshelves filled with a selection of mixed fiction, mostly crime and thrillers. The kitchen was modern and sleek, with soft-close drawers and cupboards. The utility room was functional, with both a washer and a dryer, and the bathroom had black marbled tiles with both a shower and a bath.

The bedrooms were very modern-looking, with a Swedish feel to them. Jack chose the room that looked out onto the garden and she took the other, leaving the suitcases that she'd heaved from the car waiting to be opened by the side of their beds. With nothing in the fridge or the cupboards, she figured it was time they went to see her grandparents and finally let them meet Jack for real—though she would have loved to relax in the shower first...

The drive from Blacksmith Cottage to Blossom Lane barely took ten minutes, and as she pulled into the road where her grandparents lived she thought it was a lot smaller than she'd remembered. The road seemed more narrow, the cottages were closer together, the gardens filled with more flowers.

Her grandparents' place, Gable Cottage, had recently been rethatched, and the purple jasmine around the door was in full bloom. Once upon a time she would have just walked straight in, but she'd been away for so many years she felt awkward, and she knocked instead.

When her grandmother opened the door Stacey beamed a smile at the woman who had raised her after her parents' death. Genevieve Clancy had not changed one bit. Okay, maybe there were one or two more lines upon her face, maybe she'd got a little plumper, and maybe her hair was a fine silver, but the woman herself was just as wonderful and warm.

'Stacey! My darling girl!' Genevieve threw

her arms around her and gave her a big squeeze. Then she turned her attention to her great-grandson. 'And my mighty Jack! Haven't you grown?' She stooped down and threw open her arms, and Jack stepped into them for a hug. 'William? Will! they're here!'

Stacey looked up to see her grandad making his way down the hall. He walked with a stick now, it seemed, but that was his only nod towards the fact that the pair of them were now well into their eighties and he was still going strong.

'You're looking pale, Stacey. Have you been eating?' he asked.

'Oh, you know what it's like… It's been a long drive. And the stress of moving—that's all it is.'

'You're sure?'

'Absolutely.'

She stepped towards him and gave him a hug, inhaling the scent of his usual soap and aftershave. It was like coming home. So familiar and yet also poignant. She'd forgotten it, having been away so long…

'Let's get you both in and I'll make some

tea. Jack, I've made a cherry pie, if you'd like a slice?'

Jack nodded.

'He needs to eat some dinner first, Gran.'

'Oh, right… Well, let me see… I've got some shepherd's pie in the fridge. Shall I heat that up for the both of you?'

'That'd be great, thanks.'

Her gran beamed. She always had liked feeding people. Mothering them. She and her grandfather were forever taking in waifs and strays who needed help. Even if they saw a homeless person when they were out and about they'd buy them something hot to eat or drink.

Her grandad led them into the living area and it was like stepping back in time. There was the old three-piece suite, still with the pure white antimacassars on the backs and arms. The cabinets were still filled with trinkets and knick-knacks. The circular rug was in front of the gas fire. The horse brasses hung on either side.

And on every conceivable surface family photos took pride of place. Stacey. Jack. Her parents. Gran and Grandad on their own wedding day, holding each other's hands and gazing into each other's eyes with so much love. it almost made you want to weep.

Gran's bag of knitting lay at the side of the sofa. There was Grandad's pile of papers and TV guides. A book on World War II with his reading glasses perched on top.

Stacey might have gone away and changed her life, but here in Gable Cottage time, it seemed, had stood still.

'Hey, Jack. We got you some things to play with so you wouldn't be bored.'

Her grandad pulled out a box from his side of the sofa, and pushed it towards her son. It was filled with books, toys, cars and jigsaws and Jack dived into it with glee.

Stacey smiled to see him happy. She'd missed that.

She settled onto one of the sofas. 'Can I help with anything, Gran?'

'Oh, no, dear! You sit down and rest. I've got it all in hand.' Gran bustled in from the kitchen, wiping her hands on her flowery apron and beaming at Jack, who was playing on the floor. 'We picked up a few bits from the local charity shops. It's not much, but we didn't want him to be bored.'

'It's great. You've gone to a lot of trouble.'

'Oh, no trouble at all! It's what you do for family. Have you moved in yet? Have you looked around the annexe? What did you think?'

'Oh, it's very modern. Very nice.'

'Daniel has worked very hard on it.'

'Daniel?'

'Dr Prior. Your landlord.'

At the mention of his name she felt her cheeks glow. 'Oh, right. Yes. Him.' Stacey gazed down at Jack, who'd emptied a jigsaw puzzle onto the floor. The picture he was trying to make was of a whole lot of cartoon characters. 'You never mentioned he was my age. Or so good-looking,' she admonished kindly.

Her gran looked at her, innocently. 'Didn't I? Must have slipped my mind. Can I get you some tea, Stacey? Coffee?'

'Tea would be great, thanks. We've not had time to go food shopping, so there's nothing in.'

'Oh, we've got plenty in our cupboards!

You must take something home with you until you can make it to the shops.'

'That's all right. I'd hate to take food away from you.'

'It's no problem at all. I'll put a little bag together right now.' And her gran bustled back into the kitchen, glad to have a project.

Stacey looked up at her grandad. 'Nothing changes.'

He smiled and nodded. 'No, nothing changes. Your gran likes to make sure people are all right. It feeds a need in her.'

'She's always been the same.'

'Like that doctor of yours. She—'

At that moment her gran came in again and her grandad stopped talking as Genevieve got down on the floor to help her grandson with his jigsaw.

Stacey wondered what her grandad had meant. *'That doctor of yours'*? Did he mean Dr Prior? The Adonis of Greenbeck? How had her gran been helping him? And why? He seemed a man strapping enough to take care of himself. He'd also seemed a little stand-offish, and not the kind to accept help. Especially from an elderly lady.

I must have misunderstood what he was getting at.

'Oh, I *have* missed this! Having a little one around the place!' said Gran.

'Well, get used to it—he's going to be here a lot!'

'When is his first day at the school? Monday?'

Stacey nodded, suddenly full of apprehension. 'Yeah. Same as me. My first day at the surgery.'

'He'll be all right. You explained everything to them? They know what happened at his last place?'

Memories of that time filled her with the darkness and fear that she'd begun to hate. 'They know.'

Gran reached out to touch her knee. 'He'll be fine at Greenbeck Juniors. They're good there. Nice kiddies. Small classes. He'll fit right in...you'll see. They'll keep an eye on him.'

'I hope so.'

The bullying Jack had received at his last school had sunk her son into a vast depression. His difference—a large, bright red birthmark that covered most of his stomach—had made him a target for bullies, and Jack had become school avoidant. He'd begun complaining of illness most days, growing more quiet every day, and the day he'd stated that he wished he were dead had struck fear into her heart like a knife.

Only recently there'd been an article on the news about a boy who'd killed himself due to online bullying. There was no way that Stacey was going to let a bunch of bullies ruin her son's life. He'd already lost his father, due to no fault of his own, and now his childhood was being stolen from him. She'd not wanted to run away from the problem, but she'd been so scared, and so alone, she'd longed for the warmth and protection that family gave. So she'd returned home for good, hoping that the magic of Greenbeck Juniors—the school that she herself had attended, and in which she'd been so very happy—would somehow work its magic and bring back the boy she'd once known.

'There's never been an issue at that school. He'll be happy there. Won't you?' Gran asked her great-grandson.

Jack just looked at her uncertainly and shrugged.

'It's okay to be nervous on your first day. I'm sure your mum will be, too.'

'First days are the hardest,' Stacey agreed. 'But once they're done and out of the way all the other days are much easier.'

Jack didn't look sure, and she couldn't blame him. He probably thought the new kids he'd meet would be fine until they saw him get changed for PE and then the bullying would begin. If it did she had no idea what she'd do. Home-school him? How would she do that? With her job? They couldn't live on thin air…she needed to be working.

'No word from…?' Her grandad nodded towards Jack and she knew he was asking about Jack's dad—Jerry.

'No. I thought he might get in touch when I informed him we were moving, but I haven't heard a peep.'

Grandad shook his head, totally disgusted at Jerry's behaviour. 'Shocking.'

Gran and Grandad had never been big fans of Jerry after meeting him, but they'd kept their doubts to themselves when she'd announced that they were getting married. They had supported her, believed in her own ability to make the choices that were right for her. And when it had all come crashing down around her ears months later, after Stacey fell pregnant, they'd been there again, to support her. Even making a rare trip up to Edinburgh on the train to stay with her for a week or two. They'd never blamed her. It was always Jerry.

'That's all in the past now, though. This is our new start and we're going to be fine!' she said, trying to convince herself as much as them.

'Of course you are, love,' said Grandad. 'It's going to be all right.'

She smiled at them both, overwhelmed by the love she felt for them and wishing that all her dreams for her and Jack's future would come true.

CHAPTER TWO

'THIS MUST BE JACK?'

A young woman with golden blonde hair tied up in a high ponytail approached Stacey as she and Jack stood in Greenbeck Juniors' playground, waiting for the bell to go.

'My name is Miss Dale and I'm going to be your teacher. I thought I'd take you in and show you around the classroom before all the other kids get in—what do you think?' She held out her hand for him.

Jack looked up at Stacey in question. She smiled and nodded. Jack took his teacher's hand.

'I believe his grandparents are collecting him at home time—is that right?'

'Yes.'

'Perfect. I'll bring Jack out to them and feed back on his first day, but it's all going to be fine!'

Miss Dale was bright and perky, and she

had even Stacey feeling more confident that Jack was going to be well looked after in his new school. They were taking her comments about what Jack had faced in the past seriously, and she appreciated that.

'Say goodbye to Mum, Jack. You'll see her later.'

'Bye, Mum.' Jack gave her a little wave.

She could see he was still nervous—but of course he would be! No doubt he was expecting the bullying to start all over again! He had no other frame of reference. He'd always been bullied in school.

'Bye,' she said.

She wanted to say so much more. *Have fun! Make lots of new friends! Don't be scared!* But she remained quiet and watched her son being led away, her heart filling with fear and worry.

If it didn't work out at this school…

Fighting the urge to run after him and snatch him away from Miss Dale, take him home, where she could keep him safe, Stacey turned around and walked slowly from the playground, determined not to look back. She had her own first day to start. She was due at the surgery in less than fifteen minutes and she didn't want to be late. No matter how much she wanted to stand outside this school and watch out for her son, she had to go.

Please let his first day go well.

She got back into her car and drove the short distance to Greenbeck Surgery, parking in an allocated doctor's bay. She looked up at the modern building and wondered again if she'd done the right thing. Coming back home again after all this time. It had seemed the best thing to do when she'd been stuck so far away, with her whole world collapsing around her, but was running away ever the best thing? Was going back ever the right thing?

I'll soon find out.

If Jack could face his challenges, then so could she. Inside awaited a new team that would soon, she hoped, become like a family. Dr Zach Fletcher, who'd interviewed her for the post over video calls. And Dr Prior. Both men who, quite frankly, were far too attractive and looked like the kind of doctor you'd see in a primetime medical drama rather than in real life.

Stacey checked her reflection in the rearview mirror, applied lip balm, then gathered her things. She sucked in a deep breath and got out of her car, ready to go into the surgery. Patients were already arriving. An old lady was currently pushing a wheeled shopping bag in front of her, and the doors were sliding open at her approach.

Get a grip.

This shouldn't be so hard. She'd done plenty of first days before. First day at uni. First day on placement. First exam. First GP placement. First job. She knew how to do this! But for some reason it seemed more imperative than ever that *this* first day go right.

Squaring her shoulders, she walked towards the sliding doors, her eyes falling on the posters reminding patients to wear a face mask if they weren't exempt from doing so. Inside the small foyer there was a machine that patients could use to test their blood pressure, a collection box for samples, and then there was the reception desk—a broad sweep of what looked like genuine oak, behind which sat three ladies of various ages. One was at the front, admitting patients, one was answering the phone, and another looked to be sorting through prescriptions.

Stacey stood in line, waiting her turn so she could announce herself, but then she was spotted by the man who'd interviewed her. Dr Zach Fletcher.

'Dr Emery! Pleased to meet you at last!' He stepped forward, all tousled brown hair, broad grin and twinkling eyes, his hand outstretched in greeting.

'Dr Fletcher! Likewise.' She shook his hand.

'Come through. I'll introduce you to the medical team first.'

She nodded, following him down a corridor into a staff room that was small, but perfect. Usually in staff rooms she saw chairs with dubious stains, furniture cobbled together from donations. But this staff room was bright and modern, with soft and squishy lime-green chairs, cream scatter cushions, and a low coffee table topped with a bowl of fresh fruit and a large jug of water. There was a small kitchenette with a dishwasher, microwave and—most important item of all—a kettle.

She also saw a beautiful young woman in a dark blue nurse's uniform, a healthcare assistant in a pale grey uniform, a young lady in a pale blue uniform, and last, but most definitely not least, Dr Prior.

He was standing over by the window, holding a magazine in his hand, and he gave her a simple nod of greeting. She nodded back, suddenly nervous again.

'Daniel you already know. Our HCA is Rachel, our resident vampire is Shelby, and this is our new advanced nurse practitioner Hannah—it's her first day, too.'

Stacey smiled at them all—especially Hannah. Maybe they could share their first day nerves together later?

'Let's get you a drink. Tea? Coffee?' asked Zach.

'Er...tea, please.'

'Milk and sugar?'

'Just milk, thanks.'

Once the drinks were made, and Zach had shown her the consulting rooms, he took her through to the back office, where he reintroduced her to the practice manager, who'd been in on the video job interviews, and then the admin team. Finally they went back through the building and he introduced her to the reception team.

Everyone seemed lovely and welcoming, and she was beginning to feel more at ease. Her own consulting room was in the middle, between Zach's and Daniel's. The nurse's and the phlebotomist's rooms were at the far end of the corridor.

Zach escorted her back to her consulting room, which she noticed already had her name plaque on. 'You're familiar with the operating system,' he said. 'So you shouldn't have any problems with that. But because you're still getting to know everyone we've allocated you twenty minutes per patient this first week—just until you find your feet a bit more.'

'That's perfect, thanks.'

'Any questions…anything you're not sure of…just come and grab me or Daniel.'

Stacey nodded and then he was gone, after one last dazzling smile. She blew out a long breath and sat on her chair, booting up the computer. She'd done it. She'd walked in here and seen Daniel Prior again and it had been fine. It hadn't been awkward, and it hadn't been difficult. There'd been so much information to take in, along with learning everyone's names, she'd not had any time to find her gaze wandering to her new colleague and landlord.

But he's right next door if I need him.

Stacey took out her stethoscope, checked the batteries on the BP machine, inspected her otoscope, then looked at her patient list. She had eight patients for the morning and four in the afternoon. There was a staff meeting right after lunch, and she had no home visits on her schedule for today. It looked as if Zach had had her blocked off from visits for this week, but next week her calendar for those was open. She appreciated that he was allowing her time to settle in before a full workload would be allocated to her.

She looked at the name of her first patient. Mr Elgin. Eighty-six. She thought she recognised the name but couldn't remember where from. She checked his medical history, and his current medication, and then she pressed the button that would ask Mr Elgin to come through from the waiting room.

Now she felt confident. This was the part she knew.

She could only hope that Jack was feeling just as confident, too…

Her last patient of the morning was a young woman called Sarah Glazer. She'd booked an appointment that morning, telling the receptionist who'd answered the phone that she was having bad stomach cramps that were worse than her normal irritable bowel syndrome symptoms.

Stacey had received a screen message from the team on Reception to say that Sarah had been given a glass of water and put in a side room, as she really didn't look well and was struggling even to just sit in Reception as the cramps were so bad.

Stacey went to fetch her and saw instantly that Sarah was grimacing and leaning against a wall, rubbing at her lower tummy.

Period pains, perhaps?

Sarah's medical history showed nothing remarkable. No history of menstrual problems…no endometriosis. No surgeries or injuries. The only times she'd been into the surgery had been for some travel jabs two years ago, when she'd flown to Africa, a late bout of chicken pox, one case of the flu and her diagnosis of IBS. There'd been nothing else. Could it be Crohn's? Diverticulitis?

'Let's get you through to my consulting room, Sarah. Do you need a hand?'

She reached out to help Sarah walk the few steps from the side room to Stacey's room. She got her seated, even though Sarah didn't look as if she wanted to be sat down, and kept shifting and grimacing.

'Okay, why don't you tell me what's happening?'

Sarah nodded. 'I started in the early hours of this morning with what I thought were just period pains. I am due on. But I've never had them like this. They come in waves and they're getting worse.'

'There's no chance you could be pregnant?'

Sarah laughed. 'No. I don't think so.'

'But you're sexually active?'

'Yes. I have a boyfriend. We live together at his parents' place.' Sarah grimaced again. 'Oh, God, here comes another one.' She groaned and rubbed at her lower abdomen.

There was a possibility that there could be kidney stones, or some sort of bad infection, but Stacey needed more information. 'Do you think you could do a urine sample for me?'

'I don't know... Maybe.'

'Any stinging or burning on urination?'

'No. But I passed this weird *thing* a few hours ago.'

'You're going to need to be more specific.'

'It was... I don't know. Like phlegm? But there was blood in it?'

It sounded like the mucus plug discharged from the cervix before a woman delivered her baby. But Sarah had no visible bump... *Could* she be pregnant? About to give birth to a baby?

'I'm going to need to examine you, Sarah. Can you get up on the bed for me, so I can feel your tummy?'

'I'll try...'

Sarah groaned as she got to her feet, then stopped to breathe through another pain, and Stacey began to feel more and more that what she was observing was a woman in labour. Maybe an ectopic pregnancy?

With Sarah on the examination bed, Stacey

felt her tummy, and she was able to feel, for sure, the shape of a fully grown baby tucked neatly away within Sarah's abdomen. She'd heard of these cases before but had never come across one. A woman with no idea or visible sign that she was pregnant!

'Have you been having regular periods?'

'Yes, but they've been lighter for a while.'

'Any weird sensations in your tummy?'

'No. Well...maybe... A lot of gas.'

'I'm going to need to perform an internal examination—is that okay?'

'What do you think's wrong?'

'I think, Sarah—and this is going to come as a shock—that what you're experiencing is labour and you're about to give birth.'

'What?' gasped Sarah, immediately going into another contraction and breathing heavily through it. 'No, it's not possible!'

'I assure you it *is* possible. Can I examine you?'

Sarah nodded, undoing her jeans and removing them with great difficulty, before taking off her underwear.

Stacey washed her hands and donned gloves, then adjusted the light she used for intimate examinations—and instantly discovered the baby's head in Sarah's birth canal.

Sarah was about to give birth imminently!

Her mind raced. Was there time to call for an ambulance?

'I can feel the baby's head, Sarah. You're fully dilated.'

'What? No!'

'I'm afraid so. Just stay there for a moment.'

Stacey ripped off her gloves and bent over her computer, sending an instant screen message to Daniel and Zach saying that she needed assistance. Then she went back over to Sarah.

'I've got nothing I can give you for pain relief, so you're going to need to breathe through the contractions.'

'Contractions? You're serious? I'm *pregnant*?'

Stacey nodded, almost as much in shock as Sarah was. 'I'm serious!' She gave Sarah her hand to hold.

Behind them, there was a brief knock on her door and then someone was behind her. Zach.

'What can I do?'

'Call an ambulance.'

'I'll get Reception on it.'

He dashed away, but as he left Daniel arrived.

'Hey, Sarah.'

'Doc.'

'Big news, huh?'

'You're telling me!'

Daniel smiled at her. 'Want me to call Luke?'

Sarah nodded.

'Is that the baby's father?' Stacey asked.

'Yeah… Oh, God, here comes another one!'

Stacey gripped Sarah's hand tightly as another contraction came. 'Take a deep breath and push hard into your bottom. Believe me—pushing helps.'

Sarah grimaced as she concentrated hard on giving birth to a baby she hadn't known anything about until moments ago.

Stacey couldn't imagine the shock and surprise she must be feeling. This young woman had come to the doctor thinking she was just having some really bad period pains—had no doubt thought that she might prescribe her some painkillers or something. And instead she'd discovered she was about to become a mother!

Daniel got off the phone.

'What did you tell him?' asked Sarah.

'I just told him to get here as quickly as he could.'

'Did you mention the baby?'

'No, I didn't.'

'Oh, God!' Sarah began to push again.

Daniel donned gloves, and behind him Zach appeared again. 'Ambulance is en route. Daniel? I'll take your last patient, so we can clear the surgery.'

'Thanks.'

With Zach gone again, it was just Stacey and Daniel and their patient.

'You had no idea at all?' Stacey asked her.

Sarah shook her head. 'No. I've been having periods all this time! I've been a little bloated, but I thought it was gas. I'd been on a keto diet and someone told me that could happen!' She sucked in another breath to bear down on another contraction.

'I can see the baby's head, Sarah,' said Daniel.

How long had it been since Stacey had last

helped deliver a baby? Two years? Three? You didn't get to deliver many babies whilst being a GP.

She'd heard of cases like this, but had never before met anyone who'd gone through it. All the pregnancies she'd dealt with had been standard. The mums had all known they were pregnant, they'd mostly enjoyed their months of pregnancy. Their bellies had swelled, their periods had stopped, they'd experienced kicks and babies having hiccups and eventually birth, either at home or in a hospital.

Not this. Never like this.

She was glad and grateful that Daniel was helping her. He was a reassuring presence at her side. A calm, cool and collected individual who didn't appear to be flustered in the slightest. It was as if he faced amazing and unexpected surprises every day. Just the sort of person you needed in a crisis.

'Oh, God, it hurts!'

'You're doing brilliantly, Sarah. Just keep breathing.'

'Little pushes now...little push again... That's it...one more... Brilliant...and pant! Pant for me!'

Sarah began huffing like a train, and Stacey looked down to see the head being born. The baby had a thick head of hair and looked to be full term. Of course they wouldn't know for sure until they reached the hospital and got the baby weighed and measured, but everything looked good for now.

'Perfect! Now, one last big push!'

The baby—a boy—slithered out into Daniel's waiting hands and he delivered the baby onto Sarah's belly.

Stacey draped a spare blanket over the baby, to keep it warm, and Sarah burst into happy tears. 'Oh, my God, it's real! An actual baby! What is it?'

'Take a look.' Daniel smiled.

Sarah lifted up one of the baby's legs. 'A boy?' She laughed with sheer happiness and joy, just as the baby burst into a cry, as if joining in with his mama.

Stacey looked at Daniel and he smiled back at her. She felt as if someone had smacked her in the gut. Daniel's smile was not only the most friendly he'd given her since she'd arrived, it also made her accept the fact that she was clearly attracted to him. Because her pulse had begun to race more from his smile than it had from the birth!

She glanced away, rubbing the baby, to keep him warm and to give herself something other to think about than Daniel's warm smile. Had he realised he'd smiled at her in such a way? Did he know the effect he was having on her? She hoped not. Stacey was not looking for a relationship—and even if she was, she would not have another relationship with someone she worked with! Look at what had happened the last time, with Jerry. It had been impossible to deal with when they broke up. It had made being in the workplace truly difficult.

There was a knock at the door and Stacey went to answer it, pulling the door open slightly. A young man stood there, confusion writ large across his face.

'I'm looking for Sarah?'

'Are you Luke?'

He nodded.

'Take a deep breath, Luke.'

Stacey stepped back so he could see into the room. His eyes fell on Sarah straight away and a half-smile filled his face—until he realised there was a mewling bundle in her arms.

'What…what's happening?'

'Sarah's had a baby,' Daniel explained. 'You've both had a baby.'

'It's a boy, Luke. A son!'

Stacey watched Luke carefully, ready in case it looked as if he might pass out. But kudos to him—he handled it perfectly. No sign of fainting, no denial…he just stepped right up and seemed as fascinated by the baby as Sarah was.

'Wow! Oh, babe…'

Stacey risked one more glance at Daniel now, because she knew he was watching the young couple realise they'd become parents. His soft smile was heart-warming, full of genuine happiness, warmth and contentment—and then he met her gaze and his face changed.

It was as if she'd caught him out.

He stopped smiling, looked down and away, an then checked Sarah's bleeding levels, all business again. It was as if he felt embarrassed that she'd caught him out experiencing genuine happiness and somehow it bothered him.

Odd. But okay. It was none of her business what he did. Not really. So why was she so captured by the dark chocolate of his eyes? Why did she feel that when she looked at him she was looking at a hurt soul? Why did that hurt call out to her? Pulling her, making her gravitate towards him uncontrollably?

Why can't I stop myself from sneaking looks at him?

The sound of sirens could be heard. Keen to escape his orbit, Stacey volunteered to go and meet it.

The two paramedics were young women, who were thrilled to hear the baby had been born safely, but sad that they'd missed what was usually the highlight of their day.

It felt odd to lead them through the surgery to her room as if it was something she did every day. This was her *first* day! And what a start it had been! Not something she'd ever forget, that was for sure.

'Still awaiting delivery of the placenta,' Daniel said, allowing the paramedics to take over and move Sarah from the examining bed to a trolley, so she could be wheeled out to the ambulance.

'Thank you, Dr Emery… Dr Prior,' said Sarah.

'No thanks necessary. You did all the work.'

'Have you picked a name?' asked one of the paramedics.

'I don't know…it's all still a shock.' Sarah glanced up at her boyfriend, Luke, who squeezed her shoulder in reassurance.

'Take care of yourselves,' said Stacey.

The paramedics wheeled away their patient and she watched them go, knowing she not only had a lot of notes to write up, but also a bed to clean!

Once the ambulance doors were closed, and the vehicle had begun to drive away, Stacey went back inside.

'You certainly know how to mark your first day!' said Francesca on Reception.

'I know!'

She let out a huge breath—one she hadn't realised she'd been holding—and went back into her room. Daniel was still in there, cleaning up her examining bed.

'Oh! Thanks. You didn't need to do that.'

'That's okay.'

'You're very kind. Thank you. And thank you for your help.'

He seemed unaccustomed to thanks. Or compliments. And he looked awkward.

'It was no problem. I'd better let you get on with your notes.'

And then he was gone.

She stood staring at the doorway after his disappearance, frowning. He was clearly a very confusing man. From the moment she'd first seen him in The Buttered Bun she'd sensed he was trouble, and now she felt she knew it as surely as she knew the sky was blue.

He blew hot and cold. One moment awkward, keen to get away from her, the next a compassionate doctor—calm and confident and reassuring. And all that smiling at Stacey when the baby was born and then stopping when she noticed.

Daniel had to be a man with baggage—and Stacey did not need anyone else's baggage to contend with. She already felt as if she was dealing with enough problems between herself and Jack. Whatever Dr Prior had going on could remain his problem. Because she was going to stay away.

But those eyes of his... Dark. Chocolatey. Intense. The kind of eyes that invited you to stare into them. The kind of eyes that hooked your attention. The kind of eyes that pulled at you and made you want to look within them.

Dangerous eyes.

He clearly found being in a room with her uncomfortable. Perhaps he didn't actually *like* her? Or maybe he was just one of those people who took their time to warm to someone new?

No. There's something else going on there.

Stacey had never had people not liking her. Not that she was bragging, or anything, but she'd been told how easy it was for people to talk to her. It was part of what made her a great doctor. Patients felt able to confide their problems to her.

He'd been so great at helping deliver that baby, though.

She found herself smiling as she sat down at her computer, her fingers hovering over the keyboard, ready to write up her notes on Sarah Glazer.

The way he'd calmly rolled up his sleeves, donned gloves and taken the birth of a baby in his stride... He'd kept a damned cool head on his shoulders. And what shoulders they were, too! Broad. Muscled.

He looks after himself.

There had to be a Mrs Prior. Or one waiting in the wings. Just because Stacey hadn't met her at the cottage, it didn't mean she didn't exist. A man like Daniel would never be single—she'd seen the way that waitress in the café had watched him, and the appraising looks of those two female paramedics, the blushing cheeks of the young HCA whenever he passed her by.

Women noticed men like Daniel Prior.

He'd be taken already.

No need for her to worry about him at all.

CHAPTER THREE

IT HAD BEEN a long but exciting first day. The adrenaline rush of helping Sarah give birth had lasted all afternoon, but she was keen to get to her grandparents' place on Blossom Lane to collect Jack and hear if his day had been just as good.

She packed up, and as she left popped her head around the door to Dr Zach Fletcher's room. 'Hey. Just thought I'd say goodbye and thanks for all your help today.'

'How did you find it?'

Zach was another handsome man, with a twinkle in his eye, but she didn't feel a reaction when she looked at him—not the way she felt something when she spoke to Daniel. Also, although she might be imagining things, she thought she could hear a little Scottish twang in Zach's voice. Or maybe she was just used to hearing it and so had picked up on it?

'Great! Crazy morning with that delivery,' she said, 'but…yeah, all good. Have you nearly finished?'

'I've got about ten more prescriptions to do, then I think I'm done. Got any interesting plans for the evening or are you going home to put your feet up?'

'I'm picking up my son from my grand-parents.'

'Oh, yes, you mentioned them before. Gen-evieve and William Clancy, right? I know them well!'

She beamed. 'All good things, I hope?'

Zach laughed. 'Absolutely. They're a great couple. They really look out for people who need an extra hand or just someone to talk to.'

'Gran does collect a lot of strays.'

'Yes, she does,' he said, almost knowingly. 'Well, it's good to have you finally here, Sta-cey. I'll look forward to seeing you tomor-row.'

'You too.'

She closed his door, then turned, sucking in a breath, hoping that maybe Daniel had already left so she wouldn't have to have an awkward conversation with him. She paused outside his door, hoping to hear nothing, but she could hear him typing inside.

Stacey let out a heavy sigh and rolled her head on her shoulders, then gently knocked and pushed open the door. 'Just thought I'd say goodnight…'

He looked up from his desk, dark eyes meeting hers.

She noticed he had a nice-looking room. Pictures on the walls drawn by kids in crayon. Lots of framed photos on his windowsill. Stacey noted that they were mostly of a woman and a young boy. Clearly his wife and son. Odd that he'd never mentioned them when they'd first met. Daniel's wife was very beautiful. Long blonde hair, with honey tones. Large blue eyes. A bright, wide smile. His son had Daniel's dark hair, but his mother's blue eyes. He looked cheeky and full of fun. Stacey wondered if he was at the same school as Jack?

'Goodnight.'

She waited for him to say more, but clearly he wasn't one for over-sharing. Either that, or he just liked to focus on his work when he was here.

'Thanks again for your help today,' she said. He looked up again. Nodded.

'I'm just off to collect my son—Jack. See how his first day went.'

'Of course.'

She felt as if she was floundering. He wasn't giving her much to go on. 'Does your son go to Greenbeck Juniors too?' She indicated towards the photo on the windowsill.

Daniel opened his mouth to answer, then seemed to think better of it. He smiled. 'I'm sorry, I don't mean to be rude, but I don't really talk about my family, and I have an engagement this evening that I really need to get to.'

She nodded, feeling chastised. 'Oh! Sorry. Well, don't let me hold you up.'

She glanced at the photos again, confused. If he didn't like to speak about his family, then why did he have their photos on display? Surely he expected people to mention them? If he was a private man, why have their photos on show at all?

'Something nice, I hope?'

'Dinner with a couple of friends.'

'Excellent. Well, thanks again, and I'll see you tomorrow.'

'You will. Take care.'

And so she left, feeling even more confused about this man who blew hot and cold. Those smiles of his were amazing. Warm. Inviting. Those dark cocoa eyes shone with genuine pleasure. Yet he was also abrupt and stand-offish and clearly had some barriers up. She knew she would respect them, but why did it bother her so whether he responded to her or not?

It only took her a few minutes to drive to Blossom Lane. It was a beautiful day. The sun was still out and all the flowers in her grandparents' garden were in full bloom. Bursts of pink and purple and red. Peonies, camellias, tall foxgloves. And hollyhocks at the back. There were even a few sunflowers standing proud.

She couldn't wait to see Jack. She was hoping that it had all gone well—because surely if it hadn't someone would have rung her?

She briefly knocked, then pushed the door open. 'Anyone home?'

She'd hoped that Jack would rush into her

arms, a huge smile upon his face, but that didn't happen.

'We're in the kitchen!' called her gran.

Stacey hung her bag and jacket on the row of hooks by the front door and headed down the hall towards the kitchen, from where delicious smells were emanating.

'Something smells good.'

Her gran turned, wearing a different apron from the one she'd worn yesterday. This one had a picture on the pocket of chickens swinging in a hammock and sipping cocktails. She smiled. 'I thought you'd like to stay for dinner after such a big day the both of you've had!'

'Thanks. What's on the menu?' That was so kind of her! But Gran was always thinking of others.

'Chicken chasseur, served with my world-famous butter-mashed potatoes and baby vegetables.'

'Sounds great!'

'Want some tea, love?' asked her grandad, coming in from the garden, leaning heavily on his stick.

'Perfect, thanks. Where's Jack? How did it go?'

'He's in the garden. In the treehouse. Why don't you pop out there? I'm sure he'd love that.'

'But his first day went well?'

'As well as could be expected. Go on, he's waiting for you.' Gran smiled.

Stacey felt a little apprehensive as she set foot into the back garden. It was so familiar—the winding pathway of stepping stones across the neatly trimmed lawn, the cornucopia of bushes and plants and ornamental grasses. And Grandad's garden shed, newly painted blue, with the bird house and bee station on one side. His greenhouse was filled with his beloved tomato plants, and beyond was the willow tree, and beside it the oak, in which her grandad had built her a treehouse when she was seven years old.

She had a lot of memories of that place. The hours she'd spent up there as a child. Sitting among the branches, listening to the birds and the bees as she sat upon a beanbag with her book, trying hard to concentrate on the words and not on the pain in her heart at the loss of her parents.

The treehouse had become a sanctuary of sorts. A place that was just hers. Was it still safe up there? It had been a long time...

'Permission to come aboard?' she called out from the bottom of the ladder.

She noticed that the old pieces of wood hammered into the trunk of the sprawling oak to make steps had been replaced by a new metal ladder. Her grandad must have done it.

'Permission granted!' said Jack, poking his head out from the treehouse window. 'Hey, Mum.'

She looked up at him, smiling. 'Hey, you.'

Why was she suddenly afraid to climb this tree? She could have done it blindfolded as a child, without a single change in her heart rate, but suddenly the treehouse seemed much farther away from the ground than she remembered.

And I don't like heights.

Her heart thudded in her chest as she looked down at her black pencil skirt and white blouse. She'd do better in jeans and a tee shirt, but this would have to do. Her son was up there and she needed to know he was okay.

There were just eight rungs on the ladder, and she took each one with grim determination, finally reaching the treehouse platform and hauling herself in. She looked about her and realised that somehow her grandfather had done more updates. There were shelves, a small table, a blanket and some cushions. The beanbag was gone, but there were a couple of stools over in the corner. And there was the black knot still in the wall to the eastern side. There were her initials still etched into the wood. There were the scuff marks and gouges in the floor that her grandad had made when he'd put the roof on.

'Wow. This is great, huh? You like it?'

Jack nodded. 'Gramps said it used to be yours when you were little.'

'He's right. He built it for me. But I guess it can be yours now.'

Jack smiled. 'Thanks.'

'So? How did it go?'

He shrugged. 'It was okay.'

'Okay good? Or okay bad?'

'Just okay.'

'Uh-huh. Did you make any new friends, or…?'

'They told me to sit next to this boy called Sam.'

'Oh, right. And what was Sam like?'

'Nice.'

'That's great!'

'He's deaf. Wears a hearing aid. And the teacher, Miss Dale, has to wear a microphone so that he can hear her when she speaks.'

'Oh. That sounds interesting. What did the two of you talk about?'

'Sam likes spaceships, so we talked about space. He wants to be an astronaut.'

'Well, why not? That sounds like it could be an amazing adventure.'

'He says sound doesn't exist in space. Is that true?'

'Erm… I guess it is.'

Jack seemed to think about this for a while. 'I told him I wanted to be a doctor, like you.'

She smiled. 'You can be anything you want to be. So, it was an okay day, then? And things can only get better, remember?'

'What was your first day like?'

Stacey thought of Sarah and her baby. Of Daniel. She nodded. 'It was great.'

'Did you make people better?'

'I hope so.'

'Dinner in ten minutes!' called Gran from the cottage.

Stacey ruffled her son's hair. 'What say you and I climb down and go and wash our hands and then see if Gran needs help in the kitchen?'

'Sure.'

'Okay.'

Stacey crawled across the floor of the tree-house, noting that a plank had come loose in the floor. She made Jack climb down first, then positioned herself on the edge of the treehouse platform and tried to shift herself off onto the ladder. She feared she'd snagged her skirt when she heard a tearing noise, and looked down to see there was now a split in the seam going up to her mid-thigh, where it had caught on a nail. At the bottom of the steps, she awkwardly tried to hold it closed.

'Maybe Gran has a sewing kit stashed away somewhere? Come on, squirt.'

They headed up the garden. Stacey was feeling good about things. Jack seemed fine, and it sounded like he'd had a good start, even if he thought it was only 'okay'. It sounded as if Sam could be a good friend for her son.

They wandered into the kitchen just as Gran was straining the water from her potatoes. 'We'll just wash our hands, then give you some help.'

'No need. I have everything under control,' Gran answered in her usual way.

Stacey and Jack washed their hands in the small downstairs bathroom. There was no safety pin or anything similar in the bathroom cabinet, so she headed back into the kitchen—and stopped dead at the sight of the tall, perfectly built and now casually dressed Daniel Prior, who was in the kitchen next to her gran, helping her mash the potatoes.

'Dr Prior?' she said in confusion.

Gran turned, beaming. 'I invited Daniel to join us!'

Stacey stood staring at him in absolute shock.

He was the last person she'd expected to see.

* * *

Daniel hadn't expected her to be there when he got to their cottage. Once a week, on a Monday evening, he had a standing reservation for dinner with the old couple who had been there for him since the loss of his wife and son.

Most people in Greenbeck—especially his patients—had been so kind and so patient, waiting for him to come back to work. And when he had there'd been an outpouring of love and concern.

Genevieve had called round to his cottage the first day he'd been back from the holiday that had turned into a nightmare. She'd brought him a casserole and a rhubarb crumble and told him that she would pop by the next day, and the day after that. And she had. Checking on him every day long after everyone else had stopped. She'd kept inviting him to go to their house for a meal, but he'd always politely refused. And then one day he'd felt so low, he'd accepted. Just glad not to be sitting in the cottage alone for yet another night.

Since then it had become a weekly Monday

evening date. Something he looked forward to. He enjoyed Genevieve and William's company immensely, despite their age difference. He found comfort in being with them. They made no demands of him. He didn't have to talk if he didn't want to, and often they would sit in companionable silence, or play a board game or two. It was simply company. The hand of friendship. And he knew he owed them big-time for helping him go on.

Of course they'd spoken about their granddaughter. Why wouldn't they? They were proud of her. He knew she'd had a difficult time of it, with a relationship breakdown, but Genevieve and William hadn't gone into huge detail. And he knew they'd always wished she were closer. That they could have the relationship with their great-grandson Jack that they craved. That the little boy had been the victim of bullying.

Daniel had been bullied himself, as a young boy, so he knew how that felt. It was isolating. Horrendous. His heart had ached to hear of his troubles. His healing was going to be painful, and it didn't always happen easily.

In some way, he felt he already knew them.

Only in reality he didn't. Not at all. And he felt bad having doubts about having them as tenants.

But he'd lost his wife and son, and now a single mother and her son had moved into the property at the bottom of his garden. He doubted the wisdom of it. Doubted whether he was ready to have another boy of Mason's age so close and involved in his life. He didn't know how to deal with that, and he knew that maybe he'd been a little standoffish towards Stacey. But how could he tell her it was out of self-preservation?

'Hello,' he said, looking at Stacey uncertainly, then glancing down at her son.

'You said you had a dinner to get to—I didn't realise it was with my grandparents.' She seemed puzzled.

'I should have said. I just didn't think you'd be here when I arrived.' He felt uncomfortable. He didn't like to impose. 'If you'd rather I leave, then—'

'Nonsense!' interrupted Genevieve. 'Sit yourself down, Daniel. I'll finish those potatoes. Stacey, we have a guest. Why don't you fetch him a drink?'

Stacey nodded quickly. Apologetically. 'What can I get you?'

'Juice is fine.'

He indicated the large jug in the centre of the table, filled with orange juice, ice and slices of orange. He pulled out a chair for her when she'd finished pouring out drinks for everyone, and noticed she gave him a cautious glance as she sat down.

He hoped this wasn't going to be too awkward, but he was feeling shocked, too. He really hadn't expected Stacey to be here. He'd thought she'd collect Jack and be on her way home by the time he arrived. William and Genevieve certainly hadn't mentioned that they'd asked Stacey to stay for dinner, but what business of it was his? This was *her* family. Not his. *He* was the interloper. The stranger. The waif and stray they'd adopted.

Genevieve placed the pot of chicken chasseur on the table, along with trays of buttered mash, vegetables, and some tiny bread rolls heaped in a bowl.

'Tuck in, everyone!' she said, with a huge smile on her face.

Nothing made Genevieve happier than to

have a full table. Not full of food, but of family and friends. That was what was important to her, and Daniel always went home feeling like part of her family. Would that feeling remain now that Stacey and Jack were back?

'So…how was your first day, Stacey? I do hope our Daniel, here, didn't work you too hard?'

Our Daniel. He wondered how she'd react to that.

'It went great. We delivered a baby together.'

Genevieve beamed. 'You did? How exciting!'

He glanced at Stacey, caught her looking at him and quickly looked away. She had intense eyes. The green of emeralds. Darkened now by the shadow of her long red hair that he noticed was loose. She'd worn it up at work. Now it fell down her shoulders and her back in gentle waves, like ripples of flame, contrasting beautifully with the pale creamy nature of her skin.

I'm staring.

He reached for the vegetables to offer them to her before taking any himself.

'Thanks.'

'You're welcome.'

Her fingers brushed against his as he handed over the dish and he told himself the spark he felt was simply due to the awkwardness he felt being around her. He was meant to be keeping his distance. Letting Stacey and Jack find their feet in Greenbeck without interference. Not allowing himself to be pulled into their orbit. But he was now beginning to suspect that Genevieve wouldn't let him get away with that. She seemed more determined than ever to include him.

'So, Daniel, I hear on the village grapevine that you've been asked to be a judge at the village fete this summer?' she asked.

He looked at Genevieve. 'I haven't decided if I'm going to do it yet.'

'Oh, but you must! You remember last year, don't you? The wrong contestant won. That Robin Hood costume was truly awful!' Stacey looked confused, so her grandmother explained. 'Every year they have a competition for the best dressed up baby. I think they call it costume play, or something silly like that?'

'Cosplay?' Stacey clarified.

'That's it! Well, the Becker baby won last year, and the costume wasn't even green! I tell you! Don't even ask me what I thought the judge was on to pick *that one* as a winner.'

Stacey ladled some chicken chasseur onto her plate and Jack's, then passed the dish to Daniel. He accepted with a quiet thank-you.

'Sounds awful,' she said. 'I'd hate to choose. Won't a lot of parents be disappointed?'

'Well, then, they shouldn't enter if they're worried about losing!' said William.

'They've asked Zach to judge, too,' added Daniel.

'Stacey should judge it with you!' suggested Genevieve with a beaming smile. 'Then all the doctors will judge the show. That makes sense, doesn't it?'

'I've not been asked, Gran,' Stacey said, glancing quickly at Daniel.

He saw that she didn't want to do it. And most certainly not with him. Well, that was fine by him. The less time he spent in her company the better.

'She's right,' he said. 'I think you have to be asked. Not just volunteer.'

'Nonsense! I'll have a word with Walter.

He organises everything. I'm sure we can get you on the judging panel.'

Stacey managed a smile that was neither happy nor genuine. Daniel covered it with one of his own, and changed the subject. 'This is wonderful, Mrs C. As always.'

She beamed. 'I know it's one of your favourites. It's one of Stacey's, too.'

Daniel met Stacey's eyes, then looked away. 'So, Jack, how has your first day been?'

Jack was pushing peas around his plate. 'It was okay.'

'He made a friend—Sam,' Stacey interjected.

'That's fantastic. I'm sure you'll make many more.'

Jack shrugged, and Daniel saw the look of concern and worry on Stacey's face that she tried to hide by taking a drink from her glass. Was her hand trembling? A pang of awareness shot through him and he realised he wanted to make her feel better. Make her feel more relaxed.

'There's a great Scout group in the village that a lot of the local kids go to. Jack might find that interesting.'

She nodded. 'Maybe. One thing at a time, huh, Jack?'

Daniel took that as meaning she didn't need him telling them how to live. That he knew nothing of their situation and maybe should keep his nose out of it and let her look after her son. Fair enough. But he really did think it would be a good idea for Jack to join in with the Scouts. There were a lot of team-building exercises, and it would help Jack to widen his circle of friends and develop his interests.

The rest of the evening went fairly well. Genevieve talked about the next speaker they'd got coming up at her book club—some local author that she was excited about, as apparently she'd read all her books. Will chatted about his plans for the garden and the progress of the vegetables he was growing to compete at the fete. Stacey, Daniel and Jack mainly sat and listened, and when dinner was over Daniel offered to wash the dishes.

'Oh, would you? You are sweet,' said Genevieve. 'My legs are playing me up today. Stacey, dear, would you dry for him? You know where everything gets put away. Jack?

You can help me with my jigsaw. Come along, dear!'

Daniel began to see what Genevieve was doing. Maybe she wasn't trying to match-make, exactly—because she knew what he felt about people trying to interfere in his life—but she was certainly trying to make him and Stacey friends, at least. The atmosphere around the dinner table had quite clearly shown that they weren't yet comfortable in each other's company, but maybe they ought to be? They were landlord and tenant. Work colleagues. They ought to be friends. He would try to manage that.

'I'm...er...sorry about earlier,' he said. 'If I came across as a bit...' He shook his head, as if struggling to find the right words. 'I've not been in the greatest headspace lately.'

She nodded, acknowledging his apology. 'I get it. We've all been there.'

'Your grandparents are really lovely people. I owe them a lot,' he said, passing soapy dishes onto the drainer for Stacey to pick up and dry with her tea towel.

She nodded, smiling. 'They *are* lovely.

They have big hearts and they like to see people happy.'

He agreed. 'They do. They talked about you a lot when you lived in Scotland. They missed seeing you. I almost felt like I knew you and Jack.'

'Can you ever really know someone?'

He thought about it deeply. 'I hope so.'

'They never told me about you… *Our Daniel*,' she said with amusement, as if trying to lighten the conversation.

'You picked up on that, huh?'

She smiled. 'It was quite a familiar term.'

'What do you want to know?' He turned to look at her, placed another plate on the draining rack. 'I'm not taking advantage of them. I consider them good friends. Maybe more than that. They picked me up and helped me when I was struggling, and for that I will be grateful to them for ever.'

'I don't need to know anything. I trust their judgement, and they're old enough to know what they're doing. If they want to help someone, then so be it. They helped me when I had no one. It's something they've always done.'

She was right. They had. 'You lost your parents quite young, I understand?'

Stacey nodded. 'Yes.'

'How old were you when it happened?'

'Five. I'd just started school.'

'I'm sorry. That must have been tough?'

She sighed and paused. 'Imagine being blissfully happy. Every day is a summer's day. You're loved. You have a great little family. And then *boom*. It's all gone. In an instant. The people who love you and adore you the most are brutally taken away.'

He knew. He didn't have to imagine. And he could hear the pain in her voice so clearly he felt an almost physical ache in his heart that someone else had been through such a horrible experience as he had. Her pain was old. It had happened when she was five. His pain was much more recent. But the grief was the same, he had no doubt.

He began to consider Stacey Emery in a new light, now that they had actually met.

She met his gaze. Gave a sad smile. Picked up a saucepan to dry.

'My grandparents lost their daughter and son-in-law in a freak accident at a music venue. Crush injuries in a fire. They must have felt awful themselves, and yet they opened their hearts and their home to me. And ever since then, whenever someone has been in need, they've reached out to help them, too.'

'I'm sure that having you, a piece of their daughter, gave them comfort.'

'I'm sure that I probably caused them a few hair-raising moments.'

'But they loved you. That's what's important. You had someone you could come home to.'

'They wanted me to come home after Jerry left.'

'Jerry?'

'Jack's father. If I can use that word for someone who's had nothing to do with him since he was born?'

'He didn't want to know?'

It was the kind of behaviour that intrigued Daniel. He couldn't imagine not wanting to know his own child. It was something that puzzled him greatly. Children were amazing. And your own kids? Your own baby? That was something special, and he couldn't imagine giving up that opportunity. Did they not realise how valuable and amazing they were?

'No, he didn't. We had a whirlwind relationship. I thought he was a general practice prodigy. His mind…his way of thinking about his patients was astonishing. I fell in love with the way he thought and the way he made me feel.' She gave a short, bitter laugh. 'I thought he felt as strongly about me as I did him. I began planning our future. The kind of life we'd live. Our home. I thought he felt the same way when we eloped to Gretna Green. It was fun, and I got completely carried away—which was something I used to do all too easily—and when I fell pregnant I thought our lives were starting a brand-new chapter. That he'd be as ecstatic about the baby as I was.' She gave another short laugh. 'Boy, can I be wrong about people!'

'So you broke up?' He was trying to picture this Jerry, but struggling. Amazed that anyone could treat someone he was meant to care about in such a manner.

'Yes. And it was awkward. We both worked at the same GP practice. He'd been there longer than me…people took sides. There was gossip. It all became quite ugly. Jerry was happy to give me money for Jack—to pay for him and anything he needed—but he never wanted to be a father. The man I'd thought I knew had never been there after all. So we divorced, and I moved to another practice.'

She smiled at him, her eyes blurred with tears, and although he wanted to smile back, maybe rest his hand on her arm to let her know he was there, as he would with any good friend, he felt he didn't know her well enough and it would be awkward.

He reached for a piece of paper towel, tearing it from the roll and passing it to her.

'Thank you. Look at me! Crying on my first day in front of a new colleague!'

Now he smiled. 'No. In front of a new friend.'

Stacey tucked Jack into bed, read him a story, and then turned out the lights. She left his door slightly ajar, knowing he liked to have a strip of light showing from the hall, and then she went downstairs to sit and watch some mindless television.

She'd learned a lot tonight. The biggest

thing being that Daniel, her landlord, was her grandparents' latest waif and stray. She'd heard them mention a Daniel, of course, but hadn't remembered any specifics, wrapped up as she'd been in her own dramas, and she'd certainly never thought that the Daniel her grandparents had taken an interest in was the same Daniel she'd be working with.

How she wished she'd listened! Remembered. Then perhaps she might understand him more. He'd been so standoffish to begin with. Clearly not comfortable in her presence. And yet now, after spending some time with her at her grandparents' place, they were talking. She felt a little closer to him. As if they had a new understanding of each other.

And that was nice.

Scary still, but nice.

It would be so easy to let her mind get carried away with the idea that his smiles meant something. With a man that good-looking it would be hard not to. He had those easy good looks that were so pleasing to the eye. He was a flame and she could be a moth. Drawn to him instinctually.

But his natural good-looks were coupled

with the fact that there was a mystery about him. A tragedy somewhere in his past. Why had her grandparents been inviting him for meals week after week?

'They picked me up and helped me when I was struggling.' He'd said that himself, when they'd been doing the dishes together. *'I've not been in the best headspace lately.'*

She supposed she could ask her gran, but then her gran would read too much into that, and she was clearly already trying her best to push the two of them together. Oh, she hadn't missed that! Pretending her legs were bad so the two single people could spend some time alone.

Typical Gran!

She smiled to herself at the thought of her gran trying to be a matchmaker. She'd never stopped trying to fix Stacey up. Ever since the breakdown of her marriage to Jerry, her gran had told her that she ought to get herself back out there. Not give up on finding the right man for herself.

Gran wants me to be happy, I know.

But the truth of the matter was she was terrified by the idea of a relationship with another man. Her heart was scarred. Burned by love. She'd lost her parents, and she'd lost Jerry, the man she'd thought she would be with for ever. She couldn't keep going through that pain. That loss. That grief. How many times could a heart stand it before it permanently broke into two?

Stacey stared at the flickering television screen, not really seeing the two chefs competing to be the winning finalist, thinking instead of how it had felt to stand beside Daniel doing something as normal and boring as drying the dishes.

She'd felt nervous at first, but then, after his apology, as they'd talked about her parents, about Jerry and her family, she'd begun to feel something else. Something other than nerves. Something that had surprised her. Especially when he'd passed her that paper towel and told her it was okay for her to cry because now they were friends.

Something...

She'd dabbed at her eyes, sniffed and laughed, met his gaze with her own. And he'd looked away, almost shyly...almost as if...

As if what?

But no, she told herself, dismissing the feelings. Hadn't she done this before? Got carried away, imagining things and feelings that weren't actually there? She could never look at Daniel in that way. See him as something he wasn't. Because she could not fall for another man. She had Jack to think about. And she most certainly could not fall for another colleague! Imagine the mess they'd get into when it all broke down again.

When she and Daniel had gone back into the living room Jack had begun to yawn, and she'd made excuses about getting him back early as it was a school night and said goodbye to everyone. She'd hugged her grandad. Gran. And then, unexpectedly and impulsively, she'd hugged Daniel.

He'd felt solid. Strong. He'd smelt *amazing*. And he'd hugged her back.

CHAPTER FOUR

THEIR KITCHENS FACED one another. It was something she'd noticed earlier, and now, when she was standing at the sink, washing a few breakfast things, she looked out of her window, across the lawns and flowerbeds, towards Daniel's house.

He had herbs on his kitchen windowsill. At least, they looked like herbs. And to one side there was a small green watering can.

She found herself wondering if he cooked much. And if he was any good. She liked a man who could cook. There was something intriguing about a man who knew his way around a kitchen, and she could clearly imagine Daniel in her head, standing by a chopping board, showing his skills with a knife, whizzing through an onion or some peppers and whipping up an exotic dish that would send her to heaven and…

What am I doing? This is ridiculous! I've got to stop thinking about Daniel Prior.

And then she saw movement. A shadow moving further back in the kitchen. Was it him?

Her heart quickened, she felt herself tense in anticipation, and then, yes, it was him, also standing at his sink, also washing up. She found herself staring at him. Wondering about this man who intrigued her so. Wishing she could be in his kitchen and just talking to him. Finding out more about him. Asking him questions whilst watching him work.

They would chat and laugh. They'd have a mug of coffee each and it would be comfortable. Pleasant…

He looked up. Met her gaze.

Stacey sucked in a breath, looking down and away, embarrassed to have been caught staring.

She quickly grabbed a towel, dried her hands and walked away.

The washing up would have to wait until later.

Her next patient was a young mother—Helena Farrow. She came bustling through Stacey's door, not only pushing a double buggy, containing twins, but also holding the hand of a much older child—perhaps around four years of age? And she was pregnant. She looked pale. Exhausted. Her hair was unwashed, and there were large dark circles beneath her eyes.

She sank into the chair set aside for patients with relief. 'Hi.'

'Hello, there,' Stacey replied. 'You've got a handful.'

'Tell me about it. No! Stanley! Put that down!'

Stanley had made a beeline for the multicoloured pot on the desk that held the strips for testing urine samples. He scowled and put it back.

'How can I help you today?' asked Stacey.

Helena let out a huff of breath. 'I've been feeling exhausted. Absolutely exhausted! I'm not sleeping, because the twins have me up all night, every night. I'm run ragged every day, and I just don't seem to have the energy I used to have.'

'Looking after three small children can be

exhausting—and you're pregnant, too. How far along are you?'

'Six months.' Helena leaned in and whispered, 'If I'm being honest with you, I didn't want a fourth, but my husband did, and I guess my big belly shows he got his way.'

Stacey smiled sympathetically. 'Does he work?'

'Yes. Up at the distillery.'

'So he's not able to help you with the children during the day?'

'No. He works full time.'

'So do you! Does he help in the night?'

'He tries, but he doesn't often hear the babies crying, so it's usually me who gets up to see them.'

Stacey checked Helena's last bloodwork. She'd been close to having low iron levels before, but it hadn't actually been out of the normal range. Maybe it was time to give her some extra help?

'What about any other family to help?'

'My parents live in France. They haven't been over since the pandemic. Dad's got long Covid. It's difficult.'

'You're eating and drinking the right things?'

Her patient grimaced. 'I try, but sometimes I just pick at the kid's leftovers. I snack a lot. It just seems easier than trying to eat a meal whilst it's still hot.'

'I think we should check your iron levels. Maybe your thyroid. And we'll do a full blood count. But in the meantime I'm going to give you a prescription for iron tablets. You're very pale. Start taking them straight away, and when I get the blood results I'll call you to let you know whether you need to continue. I'll just take your BP and temperature now...'

Stacey carried out her examinations as best she could with a rampaging toddler in the room, who kept getting himself into trouble taking things from Stacey's desk that he shouldn't.

Helena's temperature was fine, and her BP was only slightly raised. Nothing too worrying.

'Try and make sure you eat healthily,' Stacey told her. 'And I'll contact you as soon as I get the bloods back, okay?'

She nodded. 'Thank you, Doctor.'

'And maybe ask at Reception to see if they

know of any local children's clubs that you could take Stanley to. Just to give yourself a little break and allow him to burn off some energy.'

'I will. Thank you.' She got to her feet again, and shepherded Stanley out before her.

When she was gone, the room seemed incredibly quiet again, and Stacey found herself really empathising with Helena. It must be hard. All alone and without much family around. A lot of families with young children had struggled during the pandemic, and she'd seen more than one young couple who'd ended up having more children than they'd expected!

Stacey herself had been alone in Scotland with Jack during the pandemic, and it had been incredibly difficult. Especially as a keyworker. She'd had to continue working as a doctor and keep Jack in nursery—a place he hadn't wanted to be—as well as an after-school club. Each day she would come home weary and tired. Oftentimes made distraught by what she'd had to deal with. And then she'd have to deal with a very upset young boy who was being picked on.

She'd gone into the school so many times to get them to deal with it, and she knew they'd done what they could, but without physically being by Jack's side twenty-four-seven there had been no way she could protect him. Watching Jack's slide into withdrawal and then depression, she had found her fears for her son's health and wellbeing magnified, and had known she'd have to take extra steps.

She had eventually withdrawn him from school and returned home to Greenbeck, where there would be love and family and support and the small community school where she herself had so many happy memories. She could only hope and pray that it was still as wonderful as she'd remembered it.

Stacey went to refill her water bottle and found the staff room empty. She'd just filled the bottle, and was wiping the excess water from the lid, when Daniel came in.

He smiled at her. 'Good morning.'

'Morning.'

She hoped her face wasn't flushing red. She felt her heartbeat accelerate and couldn't help but notice how wonderful he looked this morning. He wore dark trousers and a pink shirt, his sleeves rolled back to mid-forearm, revealing a nice amount of dark hair and muscle, and a chunky watch.

Would he mention the kitchen thing?

'How are you?'

'I'm good. How about you?'

'Very good. I've got an interesting case coming in later.'

'Oh…?'

'A patient who had necrotising fasciitis in hospital. She lost a lot of leg muscle because of it. She's coming in for a general check-up and to have some stitches removed. I'm sure if you were free and wanted to pop in to have a look Pauline wouldn't mind. You'd be more than welcome.'

'Oh, sounds intriguing. I don't think I've ever seen a case of that first-hand.'

'Well, if you're free…?'

'I'll try to be. Thanks.'

'You're very welcome.'

Did he just wink?

She headed back to her room, glad that the pair of them were past the awkward greetings they'd initially exchanged and were now on a more friendly and less formal basis. But which was better? When Daniel had been standoffish she hadn't had to worry about getting too close to him, but now... Ever since last night at her gran's something had changed, and now her whole body reacted to his presence and she knew she would have to fight her attraction to him.

She really didn't want an awkward situation like she'd had before, after Jerry. Everyone looking at her. Gossiping. Pitying her. It had been such a relief to hand in her notice.

But that wink... Maybe it had been an involuntary reaction? Or perhaps just a blink. But she thought it had only been with one eye...

Whatever it had been, it was just friendly. It had to be. He was acknowledging that they had a connection now. Not just because she lived in his annexe and they worked together, but because he'd practically become a part of her grandmother's family.

Our Daniel.

She got back to her room and saw the rest of her morning patients, finishing early and noting that Mrs Pauline Ronson was in with Daniel now. The necrotising fasciitis case.

Should I go in? Or stay here?

She looked at the clock, then looked back at the computer screen. She didn't want to impose. Wouldn't it seem odd if she just went in unannounced and said that Daniel had invited her? Wouldn't the patient wonder if she'd been talked about? Stacey bit her lip, and then an instant message appeared on her screen.

Pauline's here. She says you're most welcome, if you want to pop your head around the door.

Instantly she got to her feet and stepped out of her room. She hovered outside Daniel's, not wanting to seem too keen, but she was intrigued by the case and didn't want to miss out. And, of course, it meant spending more time with Daniel.

She rapped her knuckles against his door.

'Come in!'

She pushed the door open and saw a lady in her seventies seated on a chair opposite Daniel's desk.

'You must be Dr Emery? I've heard so much about you,' she said.

'All good, I hope?' Stacey smiled, entering the room blushing.

'Of course. Daniel here never says anything bad about anyone.' Pauline winked at Daniel. 'I'm kidding! He hasn't said a word. It's the villagers! The grapevine is rife with rumours of your arrival. You're Genevieve's grand-daughter, aren't you? You probably don't re-member me, but you once visited my house with your mother. I was so sorry to hear of her passing. You had a tea party in my gar-den with your teddy bears.'

There was so much information to process in that short introduction that Stacey felt be-wildered.

'I'm about to have my stitches out. Shall I hop up onto the couch?' she asked Daniel.

'Please do. Need a hand?'

'No need. I'm not that old yet.' And she clambered up onto the couch and lay down. Turning back to Stacey, she said, 'I hear you've got a young one yourself?'

Stacey nodded. 'Yes. Jack.'

'And you're on your own?'

Another nod.

'Pretty girl like you'll be snapped up

quickly—you mark my words. Look at that hair of yours! And those eyes!'

Stacey blushed. 'What about you, Pauline? Are you married?'

'Three times! Divorced. Died. The current one is on his last legs, too. Which is why it was so important the hospital saved mine.'

Daniel was slowly removing the wrappings around her leg. Stacey could see that a lot of the muscle had been removed as even under bandages it was clear that the right leg was considerably thinner than the other. Almost all of the calf muscle was gone, and she'd had some skin grafts placed. She also had about four stitches to the side of the lower leg.

'It wouldn't heal,' Pauline explained. 'Damn thing kept popping open. But it looks okay now, don't you think?'

Stacey nodded, glancing at Daniel, who soon agreed. 'It looks very good. No sign of infection…no redness. You're healing very well.'

'So they can come out finally? Thank goodness! It's all very well being a special case, but sometimes you do just want to get back to pottering around in your garden.'

'Would you like to do the honours?' Daniel asked Stacey, wheeling an equipment trolley beside her. Upon it were placed some sterile gloves, tweezers and a stitch cutter.

'I would.' She smiled at him, grateful, and tried not to imagine too much of what was going on behind his eyes. He was being quite gentlemanly, and she liked that.

Stacey washed her hands, dried them on paper towels, then donned the gloves and picked up the stitch cutter and tweezers. The four stitches came out easily enough, and she and Daniel worked together to redress the leg with lighter dressings.

'So, when can I go back to my dancing lessons?' Pauline asked.

'I don't see why you can't do that now. But take it easy. You don't have as much muscle in that leg any more, so you may find your balance is off, or you get tired quicker.'

'Oh, it's just a slow waltz. I'll be fine. Me and Walter were doddery to begin with! What about your leg, Daniel? Still stiff?'

Daniel smiled at his patient, before glancing awkwardly at Stacey.

He had a problem with his leg? She hadn't noticed. What would have caused that?

I really should have listened to my gran when she rattled on about the villagers.

Stacey smiled. 'I'll…er…leave you to it, then. Thank you for letting me see you today, Mrs Ronson.'

'Call me Pauline, dear.'

Stacey left the room, returning to her own, and sat down behind her desk. It was lunchtime. She was starving. It was such a lovely day outside, she decided to take her packed lunch with her and walk over to the duckpond and one of the benches beside the Wishing Bridge.

It really was beautiful out. The perfect British summer day, where the skies were clear and blue and the sun shone, bathing the world in a warm embrace. She walked across the village green and noted that the benches she'd wanted were already filled. So she found a quiet spot beneath a tree, sat down and got out her sandwiches.

She closed her eyes, enjoying the feel of the warm breeze and the soft caress of the sun upon her skin. She could hear birds singing high in the branches above her, as well as the occasional quack from one of the ducks. There was splashing and wing-flapping and the occasional giggle of a young child throwing them some treats.

She hoped it wasn't bread. Bread was bad for ducks. It had no nutritional value and filled up their small tummies, so they wouldn't forage and receive what they needed. It could cause them to be malnourished...

'You're in my spot.'

She opened her eyes and looked up to see Daniel standing there, holding his own packed lunch in one hand and a bottle of water in the other. The sun lit him from behind, so she couldn't see his face clearly as it was so bright, but she felt that he was smiling.

'You're welcome to join me,' she answered, indicating that he could sit alongside her.

'Thanks.' He settled onto the grass beside her.

'No home visits for you?'

'No. Zach's got that duty today.'

She nodded, watching as he carefully adjusted his position. She thought of Pauline's comment about his leg. 'You okay?'

'Just a little stiff. It's a good day today, though. It usually gets worse when it's cold or damp. The sun actually helps.'

'Is it arthritis?' She was genuinely interested, but then realised she might be probing too much. 'You don't have to tell me if you don't want to.'

'No, it's fine. I was in an accident a couple of years back. Broke my hip. It's not been right ever since.'

'Oh. I'm sorry to hear that.'

Stacey looked out across the green towards the pond. Two swans were pushing their way through the ducks to get to the offerings being thrown into the water by the young child. She wondered about the kind of accident he'd had. Was now the right time to ask him about it? Or would that be considered pushy? She got the impression that Daniel was quite a private person...

So instead she decided to change the subject. Pick something that she assumed would be safer to talk about. 'I couldn't help but notice those pictures in your room. A woman and a child. Your wife? Girlfriend? Your son?'

And just like that it was as if a cloud had

passed over him, even though the sun was still shining bright and unobscured in the azure blue sky. His eyes became downcast and he looked away.

I've said something wrong.

'They're not here any more.'

'Oh. I'm sorry.'

And she meant it. Clearly he'd been part of some relationship break-up and the woman he'd loved had taken his son from him—possibly far away.

'They died. Two years ago.'

Her heart almost stopped and suddenly she ached to hold him and protect him, throw her arms around him and say *I'm so sorry!* She couldn't imagine surviving an ordeal like that. Were their deaths connected to the accident he'd mentioned? No wonder he acted the way he did! He isolated himself to protect himself. She got that. She did.

She didn't feel close enough to him yet to throw her arms around him, so instead she reached out and placed her hand on his as it lay upon the grass. Hoping he wouldn't pull away. She knew it had been right to do so when he clasped her fingers with his own.

'I'm so sorry, Daniel. I didn't mean to push.'

'You were bound to find out sooner or later.'

She nodded. This was a small village after all. Gran and Grandad obviously knew, and that was why they'd taken him in. Because he was alone. Knowing Gran, she wouldn't have been able to leave him on his own like that. Her heart ached. She wanted to make him feel better, but knew that any small thing she did would mean nothing against the weight of such pain.

'We were on holiday in Oahu, Hawaii. Paradise on earth. Amazing place. Have you ever been?'

She shook her head.

'It's unlike anywhere else. The people are so friendly, the nature's so bountiful, and every corner you turn there seems to be another amazing beach, or forest, or waterfall. We'd got up really early that day, to drive to this particular beach and watch baby turtles make their way to the water after hatching. It was the most wonderful thing I'd ever seen. Second, of course, to seeing my son Mason. born.'

He smiled in remembrance. Paused. Sucked in a breath.

'We spent hours there, seeing the sunrise and watching these tiny creatures waddle and flip their way down to the water, off to begin their lives, their adventures, knowing that in years to come they'd return to the beach to lay their own eggs. We were hungry, so we got back in the car to find a café that served breakfast. Another driver, who'd been drinking the night before, was speeding on one of the turns and lost control of his car, ploughing into us.'

'Oh, my God, Daniel…' she whispered, her heart in her mouth.

'He sent our vehicle down a small ravine. The car turned over a few times. We kept hitting trees and bushes and rocks, and then we crashed into a large boulder, which stopped us.'

She almost couldn't listen, but the sheer horror of his story kept her rapt.

'Penny—my wife—was trapped. As was Mason. Their side of the car was badly damaged. Crumpled in like a concertina. I'd sustained injuries to my hip and leg, and my right arm was broken too. I tried to help them, but my seatbelt had jammed so I couldn't move. I tried to get them to open their eyes. I kept pleading with them not to sleep...' He looked down at their hands entwined on the grass. 'It was too late.'

She closed her eyes at his pain. Trying to imagine being in the same situation, but thankfully unable to conjure the image.

'I was trapped in the vehicle for two hours with their bodies beside me. When the rescue team arrived I almost didn't want them to free me. I wanted to stay with them. But of course I couldn't. They wanted to get me medical attention. I needed surgery. I never saw them again.'

'So your last image of them is...?'

She almost felt sick. She pushed her lunch away and scrambled towards him, etiquette be damned, so she could give him a solid hug. She yearned to find Jack and hold him tight, but he wasn't here, so she held Daniel in her arms instead, not caring who might see, or whether it was inappropriate.

Daniel had just shared his private pain with her. He had exposed himself to her, shared with her, and that *meant* something, dammit. And she would show him that she'd heard him. That she empathised with him. That she wished she could change it for him.

'I'm so sorry. I'm so sorry...' she whispered, over and over again.

Just for a moment, they held each other in silence beneath the tree, with the sun shining and the birds singing and the quacking noises going on in the background. It felt right to be holding him. He held her back. She could feel his hands on her and it was comfortable, and normal. She couldn't actually remember the last time she'd held someone like this, apart from Jack.

Daniel was broad and strong, and he felt good in her arms. But when she realised she was still holding him, her hands softly stroking his back, she froze, knowing she had to let go, that maybe she'd overstepped some mark, that she shouldn't be hugging him as if she'd known him her entire life.

She let go. Sat back on her haunches and gave him an awkward smile. 'I'm sorry. I get carried away sometimes. I'm a physical person.'

'It was fine. It was nice,' he said softly, looking into her eyes.

'It was nice.'

Hardly an overwhelming description, but somehow it meant everything, and Stacey didn't know what to do with that. She felt embarrassed, and awkward, and she felt her cheeks colour as she looked around to see who might have witnessed her hugging Daniel in the middle of the village green!

She glanced at her watch. 'We ought to be getting back.'

He checked his own watch. 'Yeah. Listen… Thanks for…you know…just being there. I don't like telling that story. I don't tell it at all, usually. But you made it easy.'

They both got to their feet, brushing themselves down to remove any loose blades of grass that might have adhered to their clothes.

She smiled at him, waving away his compliment. 'I guess it's easier when you know the other person has been through trauma, too.'

He nodded. 'Your parents?'

'Yeah.' She nodded. Looked at him. Wondering what to do next?

They made their way across the village green, avoiding the crowds around the duck-pond, and walked up onto the Wishing Bridge. It was a small arched stone bridge that spanned the Beck Canal. A barge was drifting towards it, one man at the helm.

'My gran told me that my parents got engaged on this very spot.'

She reached out to touch the stone. Tried to imagine her mother and father here in the moonlight after having been to a local dance. Her father down on one knee.

'Really? Did they make a wish?'

'Yes. To be together for ever.'

Daniel smiled, watching as the barge drifted below them, emerging on the other side. The captain of the barge gave them a wave and a smile.

'Do you think love was easier back then?' he asked.

'In my parents' time? I don't know... I think love is complicated and difficult no matter what the era. Relationships are hard work, and there will always be a million things to tear you apart.'

Daniel nodded. 'Do you think our hearts are destined to be broken?'

She looked at him, considering his question. She'd loved her parents and lost them to a tragic accident at a music concert, when they should have been having fun and enjoying themselves. She'd loved Jerry, but he hadn't wanted the same things in life as her, so she'd lost him, too. Her grandparents weren't getting any younger, and though she loved them intensely she knew she would soon face losing them, too. Daniel had loved his wife and child and had lost them at a time in their lives when they should have been at their happiest.

No matter who you were, life and death took your loved ones from you. Was the pain worth having known them at all?

'Yes, they are,' she said. 'So we need to know how to take our happiness when we can.'

CHAPTER FIVE

'WHAT ARE YOU DOING?'

Daniel looked up from his weeding to see Stacey's son Jack standing beside him, watching him. 'I'm getting rid of this bindweed. Can you see?'

He pointed out the dreaded weed to the young boy, then looked over his shoulder to see if Stacey was around. She didn't appear to be. Perhaps she was busy in the annexe?

'Why?' Jack asked.

'Because if I don't get rid of it, it'll choke the plants that I *do* want in the garden.'

'Why?'

Daniel smiled. He'd forgotten that kids could do this. Ask why? Why? Why? 'Because that's what bindweed does. It has a pretty flower itself. You see that white bloom just there?'

Jack nodded.

'It may look pretty, but it chokes the other

plants. If you look here… Can you see how it's bound itself around the stems of these?'

'Yes.'

'Well, we need to get rid of it or it'll kill them off.'

'Can I help?'

Daniel looked at the boy. He was wearing shorts and a tee shirt. He didn't look to be wearing anything special, so perhaps his mum wouldn't be too cross if he got a little dirty.

'Sure. Let me show you how.'

And so he showed Jack how to tackle the bindweed. How to pull at the bindweed that was on its own and how to be more delicate with those bits wrapped around other plants.

The little boy knelt beside him and began to help, and they worked together pleasantly for a time.

'How are you getting on with school?' asked Daniel. 'Still good?'

'It's okay.'

'You know, I was picked on when I was little.'

'You were?'

'Oh, yeah. There was this kid called Billy

Granger, and he was the biggest kid in the year. Terrifying. And me? I was the smallest. The youngest. And I wore these thick glasses... Billy made my life a misery, but then I learned that he had a really bad home life. He didn't have the greatest background, and bullying me and some of the other kids was just his way to feel powerful for a little while. I'm not excusing his behaviour—what he did was wrong. But as an adult I can see why he did it. So, you know, those bullies you faced before... They might have something similar going on in their lives.'

Jack was silent for a moment. 'So the bully is like this weed? Bigger and stronger, but it can't help what it does?'

Daniel sat back on his haunches and looked at Jack. Such a profound conclusion for someone so young! 'Absolutely. And we have to do what we can to stop it. Use the tools we have in our power and one day we'll beat it.'

Jack nodded and smiled, pulling out one particularly long length of bindweed. 'Got you, you stupid weed!'

Daniel smiled, then became aware of a figure behind them.

'Working hard?'

He turned. Stacey.

Jack grinned. 'I'm helping Daniel!'

'I can see that.' She smiled.

Daniel liked her smile. Also liked it that it had been easier than he'd expected to talk to Jack and be around him. In fact, it hadn't been scary at all.

The next Monday evening Daniel felt much more relaxed about going to Genevieve and William Clancy's house for dinner. For one thing, he felt a lot more comfortable around Stacey now, having got to know her a little better, and he felt good that he'd shared with her his pain about Penny and Mason. There would be no more walking on eggshells… no more having that story hanging over him, knowing she would find out about it sooner or later.

He'd thought maybe her grandparents might have told her, but she'd seemed to be quite unaware of it, obviously hearing it for the first time under that tree on the village green. That was good, though. It meant that Genevieve and William hadn't talked about him to others. What he had said to them, the way he had talked to them about losing his wife and child, had remained between them.

They were good people, and so was their granddaughter Stacey. And Jack? He was a great kid, too.

He opened the door to their cottage. 'Hello?'

Genevieve appeared in the doorway to the kitchen. 'Daniel! What brilliant timing. How was your day, dear?'

He thought of his lunch at midday, sitting in the sun with Stacey, looking into her eyes. 'It was great, thanks.'

'Marvellous! Now, I know you've only just walked in, but Jack's said there's a wobbly floorboard in his treehouse, and as William can't get up there any more, and you did all those other repairs for us, I wondered if...'

'Say no more. I'll happily sort it out. Is his shed unlocked?'

She beamed. 'He's already out there, waiting for you.'

He hung up his jacket and walked through the cottage towards the back door. William Clancy was pottering about in his shed, leaning heavily on his stick, but had propped the door open with his toolbox, upon which sat a hammer and nails. Jack was trying to do keepy-uppy on the lawn.

He smiled, feeling comfortable now. 'Hey, Jack.'

'Daniel! Want to play football?'

He smiled, but inside his heart ached. Mason had loved nothing more than to have a bit of a kickabout with his dad. 'Sure. But I'm just going to fix your treehouse first.'

'Can I help?'

'I don't see why not.'

It was strange. At first he'd been so determined to stay away from Stacey and Jack. Keep his distance. But there was something just so damned easy about being with them! Both of them. He'd thought he'd feel awkward. Thought he'd find it difficult.

His first reaction had been to stay as far away as possible. They were the embodiment of everything he'd lost. But there was something peaceful about being with them. Something that soothed his troubled soul. And he was kind of happy that he was getting to spend some time with Jack without Stacey there.

When they'd first met, last week, Jack had been quiet and reserved at the dinner table. And after dinner Genevieve had monopolised Jack until home-time. When they'd been weeding and working in the garden together it had been great. They'd got a little more one on one time. At least until his mother had come out.

He climbed up into the treehouse first, then helped Jack. 'Which board is loose?' he asked.

'That one.'

Jack pointed to the centre board, which had a piece of material attached to it, as if someone had caught their clothing on it.

Daniel sat down beside it, laying the hammer and nails to one side. Jack was right. The board was quite loose and two of the nails were missing.

'We'll fix this in a jiffy.'

'What can I do?' asked Jack.

'Well, we need to get this nailed down. Are you any good with a hammer?'

'I've never used one.'

Of course not. From what he'd heard, from Jack's grandparents and Stacey, the little boy hadn't ever had a father figure in his life to teach him stuff like this. And although Stacey was pretty hands-on, he couldn't say for certain whether she was any good at DIY.

'Okay. See these holes here?'

Jack nodded.

'That's where we want to put the new nails. We'll need two of them. Pick the longest ones in that packet.'

He watched as the young lad did so.

'Perfect. Now, how about I get them in to begin with and then you can finish them off?'

Jack smiled and nodded.

'Okay.'

Daniel put a nail in one end of the floorboard and tapped it easily with the hammer, until it was halfway in. Then he did the same with the second nail, before passing the hammer to Jack.

'Tap gently to begin with. Try and make sure the hammer hits the nail square-on. We don't want them to go wonky.'

Jack took the hammer and followed his instructions well. His first hit was a little off, and his second missed entirely. But then he began to get the hang of it, and although the nail had begun to go in a little diagonally, Daniel straightened it for him with a couple of taps from the hammer and passed the tool back to Jack for him to finish off.

'We did it!' yelled Jack in delight.

'We did. A job well done! Put it there.' Daniel held out his hand for a high five and Jack returned it with an enthusiastic slap.

They both stood on the previously wobbly board and it was perfect. A little creak, but no movement. The treehouse was safe and secure once more.

'Boys? Dinner's ready!' called Genevieve from the back doorstep.

'Let's go,' said Daniel, leading the way down the ladder and waiting for Jack to follow.

'After we've eaten, can we play football?'

'Sure. We'll let our food go down a bit first, but I promise you a kickabout. Did you play at school today?'

'We played rounders.'

'How'd that go?'

'I got caught out,' Jack said sadly.

'That's a shame. But you had fun, yes?'

Jack nodded.

'Your mum will be pleased to hear that.'

'I told Sam he could come to ours to play, but Mum said we'd have to ask you if that was okay first.'

'Why wouldn't it be okay? It's your place.'

'Mum says you own it, and because Sam might want to bring his dog with him she said we'd have to ask permission.'

'Oh. What type of dog?'

'A small one.'

Daniel smiled as Jack reached the ground. 'I'm fine with it. I'll tell your Mum for you, if you like?'

The young boy nodded and raced inside. Daniel heard William tell Jack to go and wash his hands, and as he went inside his mouth watered at the aroma of the chicken biryani that Genevieve had cooked.

He saw the table was laid for five as he went to wash his hands at the sink, and as soon as he'd got the water running he heard the front door open and Stacey's voice calling out, 'Anyone home? Something smells good.' He felt his heart lift at hearing her voice. And a smile even crept across his face.

He looked up and saw Genevieve smiling back at him. 'What?' he asked.

'Nothing,' she answered, trying to sound as innocent as she could.

He smiled ruefully. He hoped the older woman wasn't thinking that he was having romantic thoughts about Stacey. He liked her, but that was all. He was in no place to begin a romantic entanglement. Certainly not with a colleague, and most definitely not with a woman and child who'd already been let down by a man. Not that he was the type to let anyone down, but he wasn't ready. Even though he liked Stacey as a friend, and had felt able to share his personal grief with her earlier today, that was as far as it could go. Good friends. She had a child to think about. And he must think of him too. Jack was a good kid who'd had a tough time of it lately. He didn't need some guy messing around with his mother.

Not that I would. Not that I am.

He watched Stacey surreptitiously as he came out of the kitchen, hoping that Genevieve wouldn't notice or think anything of it. He just wanted to see how she was after work. They did work together after all.

'All done?' he asked, placing a plate of poppadoms down on the table.

'Yes! A patient rang just after you left, worried about a rash on her baby, so I stayed a little later to check it out.'

'Was it okay?'

'Yes. Just a little eczema.'

He smiled. That was common enough. Both the last-minute call from a patient just before the surgery closed as well as the eczema.

'Where's Jack?' she asked, looking around her.

'Just washing his hands,' said Stacey's gran, as she added a jar of mango chutney to the table. 'He's been helping Daniel fix the treehouse.'

'Oh. Did he have a good day today?'

'He said he did. He played rounders,' answered Daniel.

'That's good to hear,' she said, her shoulders relaxing.

He knew how worried she was about her son. He would be too, considering all that Genevieve and William had told him about the young boy. He could only imagine the stress that Stacey and her son had been through.

'Mum!' Jack barrelled into his mother's legs and gave her a hug. 'Did Daniel tell you we fixed the treehouse? I used the hammer!'

'Did you, now?'

Stacey hugged him back, looking up at Daniel and smiling so happily he felt a little shift inside. A warmth spreading through him. He'd helped to bring this moment of happiness for them both. He'd missed that. Missed being able to bring a smile to a child. To its mother. It made him feel part of something. No longer alone.

William came in and kissed his granddaughter on the cheek in greeting, then settled himself at the head of the table. Genevieve sat at the other end. Between them on one side sat Stacey and Jack, and Daniel sat opposite Stacey.

The biryani smelt wonderful! Spicy and aromatic. Along with the poppadoms were some garlic and coriander naans, a mix of chutneys, and for Jack a bottle of tomato sauce. It went on everything, Stacey explained. Even biryani.

He smiled. Mason had been the same. He'd often said to him at the dinner table. *'Do you want some dinner with your ketchup?'* The memory hit him hard, out of nowhere, and for a moment he felt briefly winded. He'd forgotten that simple thing. And now, as he watched Jack pour the red sauce all over his rice and chicken, he was seeing in his mind's eye Mason doing the same.

'I noticed in the local paper that there's a flat up for rent. The Stowell place,' said William conversationally. 'I've circled it for you, Stacey, in case you're interested. Two bedrooms.'

'The Stowell place?' asked Stacey.

'Above the newsagents.'

'Oh. Right…'

Daniel was startled out of his reverie by William's suggestion. He knew his annexe was only meant to be a temporary measure for Stacey and Jack, but were they moving out already?

Maybe that's a good thing. I wanted distance, remember?

But distance seemed like a bad thing now that he'd met them. Now that he knew them. Now that he had begun to feel a part of them and their family.

'Above the newsagents?' answered Genevieve with distaste. 'They'd be woken every morning with the delivery of the newspapers before the sun's up! I don't think that's a good idea!'

Daniel watched Stacey's face to see how she reacted to this. Was she keen to move out? Would she prefer to stay? Was she worried about being woken early every morning? She seemed interested, and why wouldn't she be? She probably thought she was imposing on Daniel by staying in his annexe.

'Hmm… Gran's probably right. But maybe I ought to look at it?'

'You're welcome to stay at the annexe as long as you need,' said Daniel, wanting to make his position clear.

But everyone looked at him, and he felt his face colour, and Genevieve's knowing smile was rather embarrassing.

'That's kind of you, Daniel. Thank you,' Stacey said.

Jack smiled, with ketchup around his mouth.

'It's very kind,' agreed Genevieve. 'We don't need Stacey and Jack rushing into anything, William!'

William held up his hands in surrender. 'I only thought to mention it!'

'Well, maybe run things past me first,' his wife said, with an undertone that implied he shouldn't have mentioned anything at all. 'Springing things like that on people at the dinner table...'

Daniel met Stacey's amused gaze and he smiled back, reaching for a poppadom and passing her the plate.

She took it from him, taking one, breaking it into two and giving half to Jack. 'Thank you.'

'You're welcome.'

Daniel hadn't enjoyed himself like this for ages. All this time he'd secluded himself away from others, believing that was what he needed. What other people would prefer. Who wanted to hang around someone who was suffering from grief? But being with people, people who felt like family, being a part of a group again, made him feel so much more alive than he had in years.

The Clancys, Stacey and Jack had welcomed him in, and right in that moment, sharing a secret smile with Stacey that said they were both amused by the polite spat between the older couple, made him feel whole again.

He had shared his intimate pain with Stacey today and she hadn't treated him like some kind of leper that needed to be avoided—as a lot of people did when they didn't know what to say. In fact, she had reached out to him, hugged him, held him, softened his hurt with her comfort and empathy. Holding her had felt wonderful. He hadn't wanted it to end. But good things always did.

When had he last had a hug like that?

It was two years ago. The day Penny died. They'd watched each and every turtle shuffle down the sandy beach, the sun had risen, and his wife had walked over to him and wrapped her arms around him, squeezing him tight as she said, *'Thank you for bringing us to Hawaii.'*

It had been a surprise trip, for their anniversary. He'd got time off from work, arranged for a locum to cover his list whilst they'd left to spend two weeks in paradise. It had been Mason's first time flying. His first big adventure. Daniel had wanted it to be a holiday of a lifetime. A fantastic family memory that they would look back on and smile.

Instead, he'd gone through the worst tragedy in his entire life. Losing everyone he held dear.

Stacey's hug and spending some time with Jack had reached across the years, bridged his grief and his memory and reminded him that he could still feel comfort and joy, despite all that had happened.

'Jack. Slow down. It's not a competition,' said Stacey, clearly noticing how fast Jack was shovelling food into his mouth.

Jack stopped mid-chew and smiled, and then exaggeratedly did the slowest chew in the whole wide world.

Daniel smiled. That was exactly the kind of thing Mason would have done, too. 'You should listen to your mum,' he said. 'You don't want tummy ache stopping you from playing football with me later.'

'I won't get tummy ache. And if I did, you and Mummy could make me better.'

Daniel glanced at Stacey, one eyebrow raised.

She laughed, shaking her head.

And he revelled in how her bright laughter made him feel.

Stacey was wiping down the kitchen counters when movement outside in the back garden caught her eye. Daniel and Jack were playing football together.

Daniel was being so kind and so gentle with her son. Allowing him to tackle him softly and take the ball, get it past him and kick it into the goal, which had been created from two flower pots they'd moved into the centre of the lawn.

Jack yelled with delight, hands in the air. 'Goal!'

She smiled.

'They're good together, aren't they?' said her gran, who'd somehow silently crept up behind her.

Stacey nodded, blushing at being caught watching with a smile on her face. 'They are.'

'It's nice for Jack to have a male influence in his life.'

'It is.'

'Not that I'm saying you haven't done a marvellous job on your own! You have. That boy is the sweetest little boy I've ever met and, yes, I'm biased, but I think it's true.'

'Have I protected him enough, though? All that bullying he went through… He'll always remember it. How it made him feel. Could I have stopped it earlier?'

'You did everything you could. Don't beat yourself up about that. Now, then, why don't you go out there and join in the fun? I'll bring you out some home-made lemonade.'

'I'm not sure I want to spoil their fun.'

'How would you be doing that? Jack would love to have you both out there, you mark my words.'

Stacey looked at her gran, who nodded vehemently. 'Okay…' She passed her gran the cloth she'd been using to wipe up, and opened the back door to head outside.

'Mum's coming!' yelled Jack excitedly, and she felt a beaming smile break across her face.

'Couldn't let you boys have all the fun on your own!' she said.

Daniel smiled at her approach. 'Want to go in goal?'

'I do!'

She settled herself between the flowerpots as Jack tackled Daniel for control of the ball once again. He managed to take it and began to dribble the ball towards her, glancing up to check her position before he took aim. Stacey paused, giving the ball just enough time to get past her.

'Goal!'

Jack lifted his hands into the air and ran at Daniel in triumph. Daniel scooped him up and swung him around in the air and Stacey couldn't remember the last time she'd smiled so much. Felt so carefree.

Soon Daniel got the ball, dodged around Jack and shot the ball in her direction. She blocked it with her foot, sending it back in the direction of the two boys.

'Mum! You come and tackle, too!' encouraged Jack.

'All right. But I'm not very good.'

She ran out of the goal towards Daniel and

Jack, who were both vying for the ball. She didn't want to get in their way, and thought she'd let Jack get the ball first and then let him go past her. But as they both edged towards her the spirit of adventure got the better of her and she suddenly wanted to try and tackle for the ball too. So she went in. Feet and ankles wrestling for the ball with Daniel and Jack.

They were laughing, yelping, giggling, and then Jack made a surge for the ball at the same time as Stacey and Daniel, and somehow their legs got entangled and they all fell down in a heap, Stacey falling on her back and Daniel practically on top of her, Jack at their side.

She lay there for a moment, breathing heavily, a smile still on her face as she looked up at Daniel, who lay over her, propped up by his hands, staring down into her eyes, just inches away.

Awareness shot through her at the feel of him, the *proximity* of him, in a position that was actually quite intimate! His body against hers. The length of him. The weight of him. His solidness. Her breathing was heavy and she looked up into his face with uncertainty, aware that her son was still at the side of them, laughing with mirth and struggling to his feet, because the ball was free and he was going to get an open shot at goal.

Daniel got to his feet and held out a hand to help her up. She took it and he pulled her to a standing position.

'Okay?' he asked.

Stacey nodded, still holding his hand. 'Yes. I'm fine, thank you.'

Awareness was rushing through her again, and she blushed, letting go of his hand and looking down to brush grass off her clothes, in case he should see the heat filling her cheeks.

'Goal!' Jack cried behind them.

Daniel couldn't stand still. He tried to. But his mind wouldn't let him settle. He felt as if his body was flooded with adrenaline and this was either a fight, flight or freeze response.

Most likely flight.

I thought about kissing her.

That was what he couldn't get out of his head. He'd been having such a fun time. A relaxing time. Playing football with Jack. He'd used to play football with Mason all the time, so the opportunity to play with Jack and remember what it had been like had been awesome! In a way, it had been almost as if Jack was his son. He'd been helping to guide him. Showing the little boy that he was interested in him. That he wanted to spend time with him. That he was important.

And then Stacey had joined them.

Penny had never joined in their football games. She'd always watched, or used the time that Daniel was with their son to get a few jobs done around the house. Daniel hadn't minded that. It had given them a little father-son bonding moment.

So when Stacey had joined in he'd been amazed, and then delighted. They'd had a fun time. It had been relaxing, the three of them together. Nice. Easy. *So* easy! He'd almost not been able to believe how easy it was for him to be with them.

And then the tackle.

They'd all gone for the ball at once and somehow tumbled into a tangle of arms and legs. And he'd landed on top of Stacey. Not fully. His hands had broken the fall, and he'd tried to avoid squashing her. But she'd been lying beneath him, red hair splayed out against the green grass. Her laughter-filled eyes had looked up at him, there'd been a smile on her face and he'd been so close to her!

He'd felt her breathing, her chest rising and falling. Her softness. Her legs entwined with his. Their faces had been so close. Mere inches away from each other! And the thought had risen unbidden to his mind.

What would it be like to kiss her?

He'd been so startled, so alarmed, he'd instantly got to his feet and pulled her up to hers. Behind them, Jack had scored an open goal. Stacey had started brushing loose bits of grass from her clothing and he'd simply not known where to look. Towards the house?

Genevieve had been in the back doorway, leaning against the jamb, arms folded, a knowing smile upon her face, before she'd turned away and gone back inside.

'Sorry. Did I hurt you?' he'd asked.

'No! No, I'm fine,' she'd replied, nodding, looking anywhere than at him.

And it was then that he'd realised she must have felt it too. That moment when their bodies had been pressed close together…

'I'm winning!' Jack yelled in delight.

Stacey turned and laughed, ruffling her son's hair. 'Yes, you've won. But I think that's enough for tonight. Let's get you home and bathed. School tomorrow.'

Jack nodded and ran inside, still clutching the ball.

'He seems much brighter,' Daniel stated.

'Yes, he is. He's making friends and…well, I guess you help, too. He likes spending time with you.'

She turned away to bend down and lift one of the flowerpots, but he knew it was heavier than she imagined.

'Let me do that.'

'You're sure?' She looked at him uncertainly.

'Of course.'

He lifted the pots easily. Placed them back in their original position and then stood looking at her as if he didn't know what to say or do next. It was a similar feeling to the end of a date, when you don't know whether to just say goodbye, or whether you should give the person a kiss?

'Well, I'll see you at work tomorrow...'

She nodded. 'Yes. Yes, you will.'

'And if Jack ever needs anyone for a quick kickabout I'm happy to oblige.'

'That's kind of you.'

He shrugged. He wanted to. Being with Jack fuelled a need that he had. A need he hadn't realised had been gnawing at him for some time. Spending time with Jack eased the pain inside his heart.

'Well, I'd better go. See you tomorrow,' she said.

'See you.'

He watched her disappear inside the house and then he turned away and walked down to the bottom of the garden, breathing heavily, hands on his hips, blown away by what a close call that had been.

Imagine if he had kissed her! With Genevieve watching! Or Jack!

He couldn't do that. Besides, he wasn't ready for what would come after that if he did!

It was a close call.

Running his hands through his hair, he tried not to think of her soft lips, gently curved in laughter. Tried not to remember the look in her eyes when she'd lain on the grass and looked up at him as if she was expecting him to press his mouth to hers. Tried not to think how close their lips had been. Tried not to think about how that had made him feel…

The very fact that he'd wanted to kiss her perturbed him.

He didn't think he was ready for that. Because he was no fly-by-night guy. He'd never been into casual relationships or flings. He was a long-term guy. A steady relationship guy.

And there would be so much at risk, being with Stacey! She was a colleague. A friend. A mother! It would make being at work extremely uncomfortable. And this wasn't just about him, or them, it was about a little boy who had already had so much trauma in his life. He didn't need him entering his life and potentially ruining it when the relationship didn't work out.

No. I can't let that happen.

CHAPTER SIX

'HEY, HAVE YOU got a minute?'

Stacey popped her head around Daniel's door in between patients. She had something important to ask him. It was quite a big ask, but she didn't have any other choice.

'Sure. What's up?' He smiled as she came into the room and sat down in a chair.

'I've had an email this morning from the practice manager. She wants me to go on a dementia training day next Wednesday, to become the practice's dementia ambassador, but it's in Southampton and I won't get back until seven-ish that night. Unfortunately, my grandparents have chosen that day to go on a day trip to Brighton, so I don't have anyone to look after Jack.'

She looked at him, hoping he'd get the message before she had to ask outright.

He did. 'And you need me to babysit?'

She let out a breath. 'I know it's a big favour, and I wouldn't ask if I had any choice in the matter, but I saw you're not on call that night, and he doesn't know anyone else, and... Well, I trust you with him.'

He smiled. 'Of course I can.'

'You're sure?'

'Absolutely. We'll play footie...order a pizza. Have a boys' night.'

What a relief! She was thrilled. She'd known she could rely on him.

'Thank you! You have no idea how grateful I am!'

'Hey, I like Jack. He's a good lad. It'll be good for us both.'

'Thank you.' She stood, not knowing whether to shake his hand, or give him a hug, or...

Or what? Kiss him?

She'd thought about kissing him ever since they'd fallen in a tangle on her grandparents' back lawn and he'd landed on top of her. Seriously, it was as if her mind wouldn't stop putting it on replay! And then it would helpfully provide an image of what it would have been like if they *had* kissed...

It would be easier if he wasn't so damned

good-looking and if she herself didn't feel so damned lonely. It had been hard since Jerry's desertion. Going through her pregnancy alone. Giving birth alone. Raising a child alone. All the time she questioned herself and her decisions, and she missed having someone to talk to. Someone to discuss things with.

Someone to snuggle up with.

Someone to hold her at night.

Having Daniel fall on top of her had been the closest she'd come to having any physical male attention since Jerry had left—and boy, oh, boy, had it woken up her dormant desires to be wanted!

'Is there anything else?' he asked, looking at her expectantly.

Hold me. Kiss me.

'No. No, that's it. That's all.' She began to back away towards his door, smiling, blushing, feeling awkward.

I'm acting like all the other women who have probably got a crush on Dr Daniel Prior!

'Well, have a good morning,' he told her.

'You too.'

And then she was out of the room, standing in the corridor, breathing a huge sigh of relief, feeling hot and sweaty and keen to sit in front of a fan to help her cool down.

Her next patient was a middle-aged woman called Daisy Goodman, who came in, sat down, and burst into tears.

Stacey passed her some tissues and waited until she'd got control of her breathing again.

'Sorry! I just get so anxious in the waiting room.'

'It's okay. I'm here to help. What seems to be the problem?'

'I think I've hit the menopause. I'm all over the place hormone-wise. My husband says it's like living with Jekyll and Hyde. One minute I'm fine—the next I'm weepy or angry. I lose my temper with the kids if they leave a mess or don't tidy up after themselves.'

'Have you noticed any change in your periods?'

Daisy nodded, dabbing at her nose with a tissue. 'They're all over the place. And I've always been so regular. Sometimes they're really heavy, too. It's almost frightening how much blood comes out.'

'What other symptoms have you been experiencing?'

'I don't sleep! And I keep having these night sweats. This bloom of heat starts in my chest and rises up into my face. I have to throw everything off and wait to cool down. Paul, my husband, he's just snoring away, which irritates me, because I can't get back to sleep, and then I'm tired and grumpy during the day, and I'm just… I'm just a mess!'

She began to cry again, and whilst she did so Stacey waited.

'Let's have a look at your blood pressure,' she said eventually, and wrapped the cuff around her patient's arm and let the small machine do its thing. Daisy's BP was only slightly raised, and that was probably down to her being so upset.

'Any headaches?' she asked.

Daisy nodded, dabbing at her eyes. 'Yes.'

'Any other problems down below? Dryness? Soreness during intercourse?'

'Yes. Will I have to have a blood test to check my hormones? Only, I'm terrified of needles.'

'No. We don't routinely check for menopause with a blood tests any more. We go on patient history and symptoms, and it certainly sounds like what you're experiencing is menopause. You're fifty-one years of age, so it all fits. Have you thought about what you'd like to do to try and tackle these symptoms?'

'I'm no good at taking tablets, but I'd like to try HRT if I can.'

'Well, we can prescribe it in a gel or as a patch.'

'A patch sounds good.'

Stacey smiled. 'Okay. Any history of blood clots in the family?'

'No.'

'Breast cancer? Anything like that?'

'No.'

'And there's no chance that you could be pregnant?'

Daisy laughed. 'Not a chance.'

'Okay. Well, I can prescribe you a low-dose patch—say twenty-five milligrams to begin with. You'll see how you go with that, then come back in three months for a review with the HRT nurse, and we'll go from there. If you need a stronger dose we can increase it.'

She printed out the prescription and signed

it before handing it over. 'Is there anything else I can help you with today?'

'No. Thank you, Doctor. I really appreciate you listening to me today. Hearing me.'

'Of course. It's no problem. It's what I'm here for.'

'I just have difficulty sometimes in believing any doctor will listen to me.'

'Why's that?' Stacey was genuinely interested.

Daisy shrugged. 'I wasn't listened to as a child. I was very thin, and a picky eater, because food used to make me sick. My mother—a very overbearing woman—told everyone I was anorexic, even though I told the doctors I wasn't! But they wouldn't listen! It wasn't until I was thirty-five years of age, when I moved here, that Dr Fletcher listened to me and ran a few blood tests. They proved I was coeliac, not anorexic, so coming to the doctor always makes me nervous.'

Stacey let out a breath. How awful for this poor woman! 'I'm so sorry you had that experience.'

'I stayed away from doctors for all those years. I only came in to see Dr Fletcher because I'd moved to the area and he wanted to do that new patient check. He's a good doctor. You're all good doctors here.' She smiled.

'Well, it's very nice of you to say so. Thank you. And please know that you can come here for anything and we *will* listen.'

'I know you will. Thank you, Dr Emery.'

'No problem at all.'

Daisy got up and left the room, and Stacey began to write up her notes in the patient records.

She knew what it felt like not to be listened to. For people not to hear you. Her pleas to Jerry had fallen on deaf ears from the second she'd announced her pregnancy. She'd never have believed he could be like that. He was a doctor! He cared for people. She'd thought he'd be a natural at being a father—would be thrilled at her news!

Only he hadn't been. And he'd refused to talk to her about it.

She knew he'd had a difficult relationship with his parents and his siblings, but to completely blank her... To make work difficult for her, so that she'd had to move...

She'd tried to build a new life for herself

in Edinburgh, only then she'd begun to feel that Jack's schoolteachers weren't hearing her concerns. They'd told her that they did, and that they were doing their best to put an end to her son's bullying problems, but each day had just got worse and worse. Bullies were clever, and teachers couldn't watch Jack all six hours of the day.

So she'd taken matters into her own hands.

It hurt not to be heard.

'Are you missing your mum?'

Daniel crouched down in front of Jack. They were in Daniel's back garden. Between his house and the annexe. And Jack didn't seem himself.

He nodded.

'Was it a bad day today at school?' he asked softly.

'No. It was okay.'

'No one upset you?'

A shake of his head.

'You didn't eat much for dinner either.' He pressed the back of his hand to Jack's forehead. He felt a little warm and he *was* pale. 'You feeling okay?' he asked.

'My tummy hurts.'

Ah… Children often complained of a tummy ache. It could be a number of things, and most of them were not serious, but Daniel had to admit to feeling his heart race a little. He was supposed to be looking after Jack. Stacey had said she trusted him with her son, and he wanted to prove that her belief in him was solid. It wouldn't do for Jack to be ill by the time she got home.

'Where does it hurt?'

'Here.' Jack pointed to his belly button.

'Want me to take a look?'

Jack looked at him then, with uncertainty in his eyes, and said in a small voice, 'I don't show people my tummy.'

Daniel smiled. 'Let me tell you a secret. I don't show people my tummy either.'

'Do you have a birthmark on yours, too?'

'I do. But just a small one.'

'I have a big one.'

'Well, I'm a doctor. So I've probably seen every kind of birthmark you can imagine.'

Jack thought for a moment. 'Okay. But in the house.'

Daniel nodded and followed the young boy

back into the annexe, where he suggested that Jack lay on the couch.

'We'll do this only when you're ready. Just one question. And it's my favourite question to ask patients! Have you pooped today?'

Jack smiled at the word. 'Mummy says we shouldn't talk about poop at the dinner table.'

'Well, we're not at the dinner table. So, have you?'

Jack shook his head.

'Gone pee-pee?'

Jack nodded, and then slowly reached down to clasp the tee shirt that he had tucked into the top of his shorts and lift it.

Daniel was careful not to change his facial expression. He wasn't shocked by what he saw, but he fully understood why Jack would feel he needed to hide his stomach. The birth-mark stretched across one side of it, from his right hip bone to just under his left nipple. It was like a paint splash. It wasn't raised, or red, but it was large, and his heart went out to this little boy who'd had his life made miserable by other little kids who didn't like anyone different.

He rubbed his hands together to make them warmer. 'Can I press on your tummy?'

Jack nodded.

'If anything hurts, you tell me—okay?'

Another nod.

Jack's tummy was soft and palpable, and he didn't grimace or show any signs of anything serious.

Daniel wondered if Jack was simply missing his mum. He didn't know this area, even if Stacey did, and he was still getting used to knowing his grandparents in person, a new school, new classmates. And now he had been left with his mother's work friend.

He checked his watch. 'Want to call your mum? She should be driving home by now, but I know she's connected her phone to the car's system, so she can talk hands-free.'

Jack seemed to brighten.

'Okay. Let's do it!'

Stacey pressed the speaker button on her steering wheel when the phone rang from her home. 'Hello?'

'Hey, I've got a bit of a poorly boy here, who wants to speak to his mum.'

Jack was poorly? Her instincts flared. At his previous school Jack had often stated he was poorly before school to get the day off, as well as saying the same *after* school, in the hope of getting the next day off as well. If he was doing that again...

'Has he had a bad day at school?'

'He says not. Want to speak to him? I've got you on speaker.'

'Sure. Hey, Jack? How are you doing, buddy?'

'Okay. My tummy hurts.'

'So I heard. Have you pooped today?'

She heard him laugh a little.

'Daniel asked that, too.'

She smiled. 'And what was the answer?'

'No.'

He sounded embarrassed, but of course he would. He was only little, and poop was either incredibly embarrassing or incredibly hilarious.

'Okay. Do you feel sick?' she asked.

'A bit.'

'Does he have a temperature?' She addressed Daniel.

'He is a little hot to the touch.'

'There's some infant paracetamol in one of the cupboards in the kitchen. The one above the kettle.'

'Okay.'

She heard Daniel move, and then in the background the sound of the cupboard door being closed.

'When will you be home?' Jack asked.

'Soon. I'm stuck in traffic at the moment. The M27 is jammed. But I'm trying my hardest, okay? Do whatever Daniel says, and maybe try and go to sleep. Or watch a movie. But you need to be in bed by eight at the latest.'

'Okay, Mummy.'

'I love you, squirt.'

'I love you, too.'

'I'll see you soon.'

'Bye.'

'Bye.'

She switched off the phone and stared at the rear of the vehicle in front of her. It was covered with amusing car stickers and she tried to allow herself to find the humour contained upon them, but her mind was on Jack.

What if he was lying? What if there was a

problem at school? What if Jack felt as if he couldn't say what was truly happening because he knew how much she'd wanted to move back home?

She worried at her lip until she felt a pain, and then realised she'd torn off a small sliver of skin. She looked at her raw red lip in the rear-view mirror.

'Damn...'

Daniel was getting worried. It had been over an hour since their call to Stacey and she still wasn't home. And Jack wasn't getting any better. Instead, he'd said he felt worse, and Daniel was now taking a bowl to him because he said he was beginning to feel really sick.

'Here you go. How's that pain doing? Any better since the paracetamol?'

'No. It hurts more.'

'Show me where.'

Jack pulled back the duvet and pointed to the midpoint between his belly button and his right hipbone.

Uh-oh. 'Can I have a feel?'

Jack nodded miserably. He looked pale. More clammy. And his hair was getting sweaty.

Daniel began to palpate Jack's abdomen, and when he got over McBurney's Point, Jack groaned and grimaced.

'Does it hurt more when I press down or when I let go?'

'When you stop.'

This was beginning to seem like appendicitis, but Daniel didn't want to overreact. Nor did he want to wait too long. If this *was* his appendix it might burst, and he would never forgive himself if something happened to Jack. He was a doctor. And Stacey had left Jack in his care. He might have been unable to help his wife or his own son, but he could help Jack. Maybe it was better to be safe than sorry?

'I think you might need a different doctor, Jack.'

'Why?'

'Because there's this thing in your tummy called an appendix and I think that's what's bothering you. I could be wrong, but I don't want to take any chances, okay? I'm going to call for an ambulance, but I don't want you to be scared.'

'I need Grover.'

Daniel passed him the teddy bear. It was a tatty old thing, but Jack loved it. Mason had had a bear. Butters, he'd called it. Daniel still had it in his bedroom. It sat in the middle of his bookshelf, next to a picture of the boy who had loved him so much.

He pulled out his mobile and made the call, his heart racing in his chest.

Stacey received the call from Daniel telling her that he'd called an ambulance for Jack and her whole world fell apart once again. What was worse was that she was still stuck in traffic, even though she was incredibly close to her turn-off. She could see it! It was right there! About four car lengths away!

But she couldn't get to it. There was no hard shoulder on this part of the road, no way she could swing around the cars in front of her and bypass them quickly. So she had to sit there and sit there.

Finally, when they got moving again, she knew she had to drive carefully. No need for her to come off the road by being stupid.

Jack's in the best place. He's in the best place!

Her grandparents had called too, to say they were back home and were making their way to the hospital. Gran had sounded incredibly brave, but her voice had been wavery and trembly and Stacey knew that they were just as scared as she was.

'I'm coming, squirt. I'm coming,' she said to herself, over and over again.

She got stuck behind a learner driver who was travelling at least eight miles below the speed limit, but managed to pass him after a quarter of a mile, and then she was on the open road, speeding towards the hospital, where her son might or might not be having an appendectomy!

Her brain was helpfully providing her with all the things that might go wrong. Infection. Peritonitis. Sepsis… It took her a huge effort of concentration to run through the stats she knew in her head. Thousands of people had surgery for appendicitis each year and they recovered just fine. No complications.

But when has my life ever been uncompli-cated?

She managed to find a parking spot, then ran into A&E and tried not to burst with frustration as she stood in a queue waiting to get to the reception desk.

'Stacey?'

She turned, and there was her grandad, over by the vending machine, waiting for it to deliver a cup of what would no doubt be questionable tea.

'I thought it was you, love. Your gran's in a state. I thought a tea might calm her nerves, and I said I'd pop down to see if you were here.'

'How's Jack?'

'He's been taken for surgery.'

'What? Why didn't anyone call me?'

'There wasn't time, love. They thought his appendix might have burst, so they just rushed him in. Terrifying, it is.' He took her arm. 'Let me take you up to the ward.'

She nodded, and walked patiently beside her grandfather, wishing he would walk faster, but knowing his limitations. If Jack was in surgery already there was no point in rushing anyway. Whether she arrived on the surgical ward in the next five minutes or twenty-five minutes would make no difference to Jack. He wouldn't be there.

She tried not to think of him in surgery. Her poor little boy all alone on the table.

Up on Shelley Ward, in a family waiting room, her gran was pacing the floor, and seated on a green plastic chair, staring forlornly at the floor, was Daniel.

'Look who I found,' said her grandad.

They both looked up. She saw tears form in her grandmother's eyes and a huge look of relief on Daniel's face.

'Any news from Theatre?'

'No, nothing,' said her gran, gratefully accepting the cup of tea from her husband, taking a sip and wincing at the heat.

Daniel had got up. He was by her side, his hand on her arm. 'Are you okay?' he asked.

She was grateful for his concern. 'Yes. Scared, though.'

'Of course. I know exactly how you feel,' he answered quietly, his eyes clouding over.

'Did they say how long it might be?'

'No. But a very nice nurse said she'll come out to update us when she can,' said her gran.

'Here, take a seat,' suggested Daniel, and she sank into one of the ugly green seats beside him.

It felt wrong to just be sitting there. Doing nothing. This was her son, and he needed help, and she had to rely on other doctors, people she didn't know, to save his life. It was the most impotent she'd ever felt in her whole life. Tears began to fall, and her gran passed her a tissue from the depths of her handbag.

'We've had such a wonderful day in Brighton,' said her gran. 'To come back to this...' She shook her head, almost in disbelief.

'I know...' said Stacey. 'I feel so useless.'

Daniel reached out and took her hand. Squeezing it. Holding it. Just letting her know that he was there. That he understood.

Of course he did. He'd been stuck in a car, unable to move, unable to help his wife and child. He'd watched them die!

I could never be that strong.

She leant into him, rested her head on his shoulder without thinking. It felt right. It felt like what she needed. Just a moment of support from someone whom she knew was probably as terrified as she was. He knew how scared she must be. How lost she felt.

'This tea is terrible!' Her gran winced after

taking another sip. 'And now I need the loo. Where are the toilets?'

'There are some just outside the ward. Want me to show you? I could do with a tinkle as well,' said her grandad, and he took his wife's hand and they ambled off, leaving Daniel and Stacey alone.

'I feel I should be doing more. Should I be calling someone?' she asked, her mind whizzing with thoughts.

'Like who? All his family is here.'

She was silent for a moment. Thinking of Jerry. 'Not all of them.'

She felt Daniel reach for his mobile. He handed it to her. 'If you need to call him, then do.'

She lifted her head to look at him. 'No, he's never wanted anything to do with Jack.'

She swallowed hard, suddenly immensely sad for her son. Guilty that she hadn't managed to give him a father. Hadn't managed to hold on to her husband. Hadn't managed to keep Jack safe.

Her heart ached.

She looked up into Daniel's face, searching for answers, for clues as to how he'd got himself through such an ordeal. How she was meant to deal with this! But instead she found herself getting lost in those deep brown eyes of his. Daniel was looking down at her with such concern, with such intensity, with such...longing...

She felt it too. That need to reach out and find comfort from another human being. That need to feel that you had a soft place to fall when all around you the world was sharp with shards of brittle glass.

His face was so close to hers. They were so close to each other. Her hand was still in his. Her body was turned to his. Her heart was racing. Her breathing much faster as she contemplated accepting the comfort she would find in him.

All it would take would be for her to edge closer.

She looked down at his lips. Saw that they were parted. Expectant. Waiting. Longing. She yearned to press her mouth to his, to give in to the attraction she felt, the need she wanted to feed, to embrace Daniel...

'Are you Jack's parents?'

The voice intruded, breaking the fantasy

she had begun to believe might finally come true and thrusting reality back into her face.

They broke apart as Stacey turned and stood, releasing Daniel's hand. 'I'm Jack's mother.'

'The surgery went well. He's in Recovery. Would you like to come and see him?'

Oh, the relief!

'Thank you! Thank you so much!'

Stacey turned to Daniel, but it was like looking at a different man. He'd stepped back, looking guilty, and now he could barely meet her gaze.

She wanted to tell him that it was okay.

But she needed to see Jack more.

Jack lay in his hospital bed holding his tatty teddy. A drip was attached to his arm, and although he still looked pale, he looked a lot better. Seeing his pain increase had made Daniel feel awful.

Stacey had hurried to her son's side and Jack's face lit up at seeing her.

'Hey, squirt!' she said, taking hold of his hand as she bent over the bed to press a kiss to his forehead. 'How are you feeling?'

'I'm okay.'

'Any pain?' Stacey looked Jack up and down.

'No. Not any more.'

'That's good.'

'Where's Daniel?'

Stacey turned to look at him and Daniel gave her an awkward smile and stepped forward, so that Jack could see him too. 'I'm here.'

The little boy smiled and closed his eyes, drifting off again into the land of nod.

Daniel stood opposite Stacey, still trying to figure out what had just happened out in the waiting area of Shelley Ward.

There'd been a moment.

That was the only way he could describe it.

Stacey had been resting her head on his shoulder and she'd looked up at him and...

He swallowed. 'Do you think we should talk about what happened out there?' he asked in a low voice.

Stacey blushed and turned to look at Jack, but he was fast asleep. 'Nothing happened.'

'But it nearly did. You were going to... I mean, I was going to... And then that nurse arrived.'

'This isn't the place, Daniel,' she whispered.

He looked at Jack, still sleeping. 'No. Maybe not.'

Behind them, Stacey's grandparents suddenly arrived, masked and gowned. 'The nurses said we could have five minutes. Just to see him. And then we've got to come back out.'

'He's okay. Still sleepy,' Stacey said, glancing over at Daniel.

She looked angry. But what did she have to be angry about? Was she angry with him? Or herself? Clearly she thought that whatever *hadn't* happened between them had been a mistake.

And maybe she was right.

'I'll go,' he volunteered. 'You and William stay, Genevieve.'

Mrs Clancy looked over at him in gratitude and surprise. 'Are you sure?'

'Of course. He's your grandson. I'll wait outside.'

And he strode away from the bed and went back out into the corridor, sighing heavily, still feeling distraught. He'd been so scared, watching Jack deteriorate. He'd witnessed that before. Trapped in a car with his wife and son, unable to help either of them, he'd watched the life slowly leave their eyes, screaming in frustration and grief. To witness it again, with Stacey's little boy, whom he'd been left in charge of...he couldn't let it happen.

He'd done the right thing.

But that moment...

He couldn't get the image out of his head. How Stacey had looked up into his eyes. How it had made him feel!

Excited. Terrified. Wanting. Doubt. Fear.

Adrenaline had rushed through him and he'd debated whether to press his lips to hers or not. This was a stressful situation...they were only in it because of Jack. Would it have happened anywhere else? In any other situation?

Maybe.

He'd been fighting his attraction to her ever since she'd arrived, and he'd got the feeling that maybe she was doing the same thing, too.

They needed to talk.

Daniel paced the corridor, back and forth, back and forth, so much so that he thought he'd wear a rut in the floor. Suddenly the doors opened and William and Genevieve came out, smiling.

'He's asking for you.'

He looked from one old friend to another. 'Oh, I'm not sure I should interfere—'

'Nonsense! He wants to see you. You go on in.'

He nodded, then used the hand gel on the wall and cleaned his hands once again before going back in and moving towards Jack's bed.

Stacey was where she'd been before. Sitting by her son's bed, still holding his hand. But this time, Jack looked a little more awake. The boy even smiled.

'Daniel!'

'Hey…you're looking much better.'

'Thank you.'

'No problem.'

'Thank you for looking after me when I got poorly.'

'My pleasure.'

'When I get out of here, maybe we can play football again?'

'Daniel might be busy,' Stacey said, not looking at him.

Was she trying to tell him to stay away? Maybe he should. He didn't need to be getting involved with these two. He should have stuck to his first impression and stayed away. Not got involved.

'We'll see. When you're better.'

He glanced at Stacey, but she refused to meet his eyes. Okay. That was fine. He got the message.

'I'd better let you rest.'

'Stay? Please?' Jack whined, letting go of Grover to hold up his left hand for Daniel to take.

How could he refuse?

So Daniel stepped forward, sat down on the other chair and took Jack's hand.

The little boy smiled and drifted off to sleep again.

Stacey kept her gaze fixed on her son.

Daniel decided to stay quiet and do exactly the same thing.

It was fine.

He didn't want to go to dinner the following Monday evening. Anyway, it was his turn to be the duty doctor, and he also had a home visit booked in. So he called the Clancy house and Will picked up.

'Hello?'

'Hey, it's Daniel.'

'Ah! Our hero! How are you?'

He didn't feel like a hero, but he skipped over that. 'I'm great. Listen, I thought I'd better give you a quick call. I've got a home visit to do tonight after surgery, and then I'm on call, so I won't be popping round for dinner.'

'Oh! That's a shame! I know Gen was hoping to cook you something special—you know, as a thank-you for what you did with Jack.'

'There's no need.'

'Nonsense! What will you do for food tonight? Probably grab a sandwich from the store, I'm guessing. Look, I'll get Gen to do you a plate and you can pop in your way home and take it back with you…heat it up in the microwave.'

'Oh, I really don't want her to go to any trouble…'

'You're family, Daniel, it's no trouble. You know she likes to keep you well fed! Do me a favour and give me a night off from her worrying and fretting about you not looking after yourself properly. Accept the meal.'

He smiled. 'All right. But it'll be a flash visit.'

'Perfect.'

When he arrived at the Clancy house that evening he sat in the car for a brief while, just breathing in and out, trying to psych himself up for seeing Stacey. She'd not been at work since last week, when Jack had got his appendicitis, because she was looking after him, but he assumed she'd be at her grandparents' place today—as she had been the last few Monday evenings.

Once he felt ready, he made his way up the garden path, ready with a mouthful of excuses as to why he couldn't stay so that he didn't make it awkward for Stacey. Or himself! But when he made it inside he discovered only William and Genevieve at the kitchen table.

'They're not here, if you're wondering,' said Genevieve.

'Jack's still resting at home,' said William, closing his newspaper and getting up to reach for a tray upon which sat a covered plate of food. 'It's still hot, if you've got time to eat it here?'

'No. Thank you. My patient is expecting me.' Daniel accepted the plate, wrapped in a towel to keep it warm.

'Everything all right between you and Stacey?' asked Genevieve, curiosity soaking her words.

He nodded, smiling. 'Fine!'

'You don't seem fine. She doesn't blame you, you know.'

'Blame me?'

'For Jack getting appendicitis. She knows it would have happened whether she was there or not.'

'I know, and everything's fine.'

'Hmm… That's what she said.' Genevieve pursed her lips, clearly not believing either one of them. 'You know you can talk to us about anything, Daniel. We're here for you. We always have been.'

'I know, and I'm very grateful for how you've looked after me since…since I lost Penny and Mason.'

She nodded and got up to give him a quick

hug. 'All right. Well, you'd better be off, if you're in a rush.'

'I am.'

He thanked them once again and went back out to his car, laying the plate down in the footwell of the vehicle and hating himself for lying to them. But what could he have said?

Your granddaughter and I nearly kissed. Only we didn't, and then it got awkward.

Daniel started the engine and set off to see his home visit patient.

CHAPTER SEVEN

STACEY RETURNED TO work the same day Jack returned to school. She'd enjoyed having time with him at home.

Just as she'd been getting ready, pulling on a navy skirt, her gran had rung to tell her that she'd seen Walter, who was in charge of the village fete, and he'd agreed that Stacey could judge the baby fancy dress competition, alongside Zach and Daniel.

Her heart had sunk. That would mean pasting a smile on her face and hoping that everyone thought she was having a whale of a time!

Maybe I could stick close to Zach? Interact with him?

It had been easy to avoid Daniel over the last few days. He'd been at work for most of them, except the weekend, and she'd kept the curtains of the annexe closed, lowered the blinds at the kitchen window and enjoyed movie marathon days with her son and a few bowls of popcorn.

Jack was recovering brilliantly. He'd been a bit scared of getting up and walking around at first, but when he'd realised that there wasn't any pain—due to the strong painkillers he'd been given—his recovery had come on much faster, and a few nights ago—much to her intense surprise—he'd started asking about when he could return to school?

'I miss Sam. And George. And Toby!'

She'd laughed, delighted at this turn of events. Despite the drama with Daniel, perhaps moving here *had* been the best thing for her son?

When she got to the surgery, after dropping Jack off at school, she hurried straight to her room and closed the door behind her. She was hoping to just get on with her morning list and go and eat her lunch somewhere, without being spotted by Daniel, then finish her afternoon list and go home.

Only she wasn't that lucky.

Knuckles rapped on her door.

'Come in,' she said, hoping fervently that

it was Hannah, or Zach, or a member of staff from Reception.

But it was Daniel.

Her heart began to thud painfully in her chest so she sat behind her desk, logging into the system after inserting her NHS card into the computer.

'We need to talk,' he said.

'Do we?' She kept her eyes fixed on the screen.

'Yes. We do. Talk about what happened.'

'Now isn't the time, Daniel.'

'Then when is? Because you wouldn't let me talk at the hospital, and you've avoided me all the time whilst Jack has been recovering. I knocked on your door at the weekend. I knew you were in there, but you didn't answer.'

She'd heard it. Wondered if it had been him and guiltily ignored it. 'I'm sorry. I didn't hear you.'

Daniel sank into the patient's chair beside her desk. 'We're adults. Let's deal with this. Nothing happened between us—there's no reason we can't just be friends.'

She looked up at him then. Not believing him. 'It's that easy?'

'Yes!' he said, exasperated. 'It has to be. Listen, I was just as shocked as you at what nearly happened, and it freaked me out too. Believe me, I don't need to develop feelings for you and Jack, because all I can think of is what will happen when it ends. I'm so scared of how I'll feel if it all goes wrong that I can't even contemplate letting it *start*. So…friends only. Okay?'

She listened to his words. Shocked. Surprised. She wasn't used to guys telling her the truth up-front. She was used to awkward silences, refusals even to discuss anything important, and then eventual desertion. This frankness and honesty was surprising! And actually quite nice. She really ought not to have suspected he'd be like Jerry.

'You're right. I've been feeling the same way.'

'You have?' He sounded unsure.

She nodded. 'I've been in a relationship with another GP in the same practice and it didn't work out well for me when it ended—so, yes, I kept thinking that my life would end up the same. And I'd have to leave here. Leave just as everything is getting good! Maybe I'm pessimistic, but when you've had your entire life turned upside down by a romantic relationship, it makes you terrified of the next one!'

He stared at her. 'I don't ever want you to feel that you would have to leave.'

'Well, you haven't. Not yet.' She smiled at him, trying to inject a bit of humour into a fraught moment.

'So, we continue as we are? Just friends?'

'Just friends.' She held out her hand so that they could shake on it.

He took her hand in his.

She kept the smile on her face, ignoring the thrill that ran up her arm and ignoring the way her body still reacted to him. She would teach it. Teach it to expect nothing from this man. They had established clear parameters for their relationship. It was the most grown-up she'd felt in ages.

He let go. 'Okay. I'll see you later?'

'You will.' She watched him go, letting out a huge breath of relief once he was out of earshot.

* * *

Daniel initially felt much better, having spoken to Stacey, and was glad that he'd taken Zach's advice on the matter. He'd met Zach first thing that morning, asked if he could have a quick word, and Zach had invited him to share. His best friend had listened well and told him just to be honest with Stacey.

It turned out that Zach—whom Daniel knew had secret feelings for Hannah, the new advanced nurse practitioner—wanted to tell Hannah how he felt, but knew how much pressure that would put on her after what had happened to her in a past relationship. He didn't want to scare her off. But he thought that because Daniel and Stacey weren't even involved yet, they should talk. Set the record straight.

Which he'd done.

He'd been terrified, but he'd done it. Even if it wasn't exactly true about them not being involved yet. He *felt* involved, and that was why he had to pull away. He was becoming entwined with her family and her history. He'd practically been adopted by her grandparents. He'd babysat Jack. Cared for him when he was sick. Worked with Stacey. Sat and told her of his painful past on the village green. And she'd sat and listened to him, her eyes full of empathy and support. They'd eaten meals together. Washed dishes together. Laughed. Joked. Rolled on the grass together. Been happy.

And then, at the hospital, had come that moment in which they'd almost kissed…

He had to pull free of her. It was the only way to secure the safety of his heart.

So why do I feel so rubbish?

He told himself the bad feeling would pass. That it was a feeling he could deal with. This disappointment. This sadness. It would be easy enough. It wasn't the heart-stopping brutality of utter grief and loss. That was what he was trying to avoid.

I'm doing the right thing.

His first patient of the day was Brooke Miller, a young woman of twenty-six, who sat down in front of him with a nervous smile.

'Morning,' he said. 'How can I help you today?'

'I want to quit smoking. I've tried before.

Tried doing it on my own. But I wasn't strong enough so I think I need some proper advice.'

'Well, usually I ask a patient what their motivation is. If the motivation is strong, then that's a good foundation to start.'

'I want a baby. Me and my partner Jacob… we want to start a family. But I'm worried about the effect of smoking on my pregnancy.'

'Okay. That's a great reason!' Daniel smiled, diving into his desk drawer to pick out the stop smoking literature he had in there, which listed support groups and their telephone numbers, as well as helpful websites that Brooke could visit. 'How many do you smoke a day?'

'About twenty.'

'And what did you try before? Just willpower?'

'Yeah.' She nodded. 'And chomping on mints and sweets. But then I just got fat and broke out in spots. And that would be okay for me if I was pregnant, but not when I was actually trying to seduce my partner, you know?' She giggled and blushed.

Daniel smiled. 'How about we prescribe you some nicotine patches and gum? The gum is sugarless, and it really helps in conjunction with the patches.'

She nodded. 'Sounds great. I think I have an addictive personality. My willpower isn't that great either, so I need all the help I can get.'

'Well, give these a try and come back and see me in about a month.'

'Thanks.' She took the prescription. 'It's just so hard, you know? When you want something so bad and you know what you have to do to achieve it, but you just can't bring yourself to do it... It seems so big. Too hard. Scary. It's easy to give in and not try, right? The easier road?'

He stared at her and nodded. 'Maybe everything that's worth having is worth fighting for?'

Brooke smiled. 'It is. It truly is. Thanks, Dr Prior.'

And she was gone.

Daniel thought of her words and then his own.

He knew staying away from Stacey and Jack was the easier road. The safer road. But he also knew that they were the type of people worth fighting for.

He just knew he didn't have it in him to do the fighting.

It was Hannah, the advanced nurse practitioner, who told Stacey about the house for sale.

She knew she had to find somewhere. There was definitely no way she could stay at the annexe—it was too distracting. Just the other night she'd been standing at the kitchen sink, washing a few dishes, and hadn't been able to help but notice Daniel doing the same thing. She'd begun to stare at him. Aware of the vast space between them that she felt unable to cross. Wondering what he was thinking. Whether he was struggling with this just as much as she was.

She had begun to dream of him now, and it was frustrating to have him so near and yet so far.

And then later, after she'd put Jack to bed, she'd grabbed herself a nice glass of wine and happened to notice Daniel in his garden, on his patio, head down, reading a book. How long he'd been there she didn't know, but wouldn't you know it? He glanced up and looked at the annexe right at that moment. She'd jumped back out of view, in case he caught her looking, and then frantically worried about whether he'd seen her watching him or not!

So, no, staying at the annexe was too difficult. But now that she was looking around the completed show home at the new development being built on the outskirts of Greenbeck, she wasn't sure how she'd feel about leaving it either.

The show home was beautiful. As all the houses obviously would be. The best interior decorators had clearly played their hands here. Everything was tasteful, yet somehow decadent, and the agent had allowed her to look around by herself, after he'd given her a detailed tour.

It would make someone a lovely home, but was it the right sort of place for her and Jack?

She sucked in a breath as she stood in one of the bedrooms of the house and looked out across the building site. The houses were in various states of construction and there were workmen everywhere. She tried to imagine it as a new estate. With all the families that would eventually move in. All the new patients who would ask to be taken on at the surgery.

Could she live here?

There were designs in the plans showing a community park in the centre, with a playground for little ones, which would be nice. And the developers were clearly trying to keep it as green as they could as they intended to plant lots of new trees, too, and create a rewilding centre to encourage butterflies and bees and local wildlife, which was excellent.

But was it home?

She was biting her lip, worrying about what to do, when the agent came running up the stairs shouting for her.

'Dr Emery?'

'Yes?'

'I'm sorry to bother you, but we might be in need of your expertise.'

She frowned. 'How do you mean?'

'One of the carpenters has had an accident. There's a hand injury, I believe. Any chance you could take a look?'

She nodded, smiled. 'Sure. Of course.'

This happened a lot when she went out. If people knew she was a doctor, and there was an incident, she was often called. She had no equipment with her, and she wasn't at the surgery, so she wasn't sure how much help she'd be, but...

She followed the agent through the front doors and he led her to a Portakabin to the left of the new estate, where a young man sat with his hand wrapped in a towel.

'What happened?'

'I tripped over some lumber and put my hands out to stop the fall. I landed on a saw. I'm sure it's superficial. Looks a lot worse than it is. I've told these guys I'm fine.'

She smiled. 'Let me be the judge of that. Can I have a look?'

He nodded and she unwrapped the towel and found quite an injury across the base of the man's palm. Another inch or two and the serrated edge of the saw would have cut into his wrist, where all the delicate and important nerves and arteries ran. As it was, he'd need the wound to be cleaned and he would require stitches.

'You can feel me touching you here?' she asked. 'And here?' She lightly grazed his palm and fingers with her own.

'Yeah.'

She checked his capillary refill. That looked fine. 'I'm not sure you'll need plastic surgery or a hand surgeon, but you do need to go to hospital for stitches.'

He frowned. 'You sure?'

'The wound needs to be cleaned properly, for a start. Are you up on your tetanus shots?'

'I don't know.'

'Well, you'll need that to be checked too.'

'You can't do it for me at the surgery?'

'We're not a minor injuries unit, I'm afraid. We don't do walk-ins. We're not equipped for that.'

'Okay. All right. Thanks, Doc.'

'You're welcome.'

She headed for home, armed with a brochure for the new houses, and as she walked down the side of Daniel's house to head to the annexe, where her gran was looking after Jack, she met Daniel, who was just bringing a bag of rubbish out to his bin.

She smiled awkwardly. 'Hi.'

'Hi.'

She saw his gaze drop down to the bro-chure and for a brief moment he looked puz-zled, hurt. But then he brightened and forced a smile. 'House-hunting?'

She shrugged. 'Oh, you know... Keeping my options open. We can't impose on you for ever.'

'It's not a problem. I've told you—stay for as long as you need.'

'That's kind of you.'

'See anything you like?'

What?

She blushed, then realised he was talking about the houses on the new estate. 'Oh... erm...you know what these places are like. Expensive. Perfect. But are they home? I don't know. I think I'm looking for a place with a bit more...heart.'

He nodded. 'I get that.'

She stood looking at him a moment more, realising she couldn't think of one more word to say to him. But then she said, 'I'll be help-ing you judge that baby fancy dress competi-tion at the village fete, after all.'

'Oh?'

'Yes.' She laughed self-consciously. 'Gran twisted that guy's arm. Walter?'

He nodded. 'Great. I look forward to it. How's Jack?'

'Doing well still. Back at school.'

'That's great. It's good for him to be back to normal.'

'It is!'

Another awkward silence descended and Stacey simply didn't know what to do. Staying away from Daniel had been hard, and she'd missed their casual chats. Even Jack had noticed that he hadn't seen Daniel for a while, and had asked her when they could next play football. And it was also hard standing there, looking at this man she felt so many things for, pretending that everything was fine and that they were just friends, when there was an underlying tension between them.

'You've remembered it's Shelby's birthday tomorrow?' he said.

Shelby...the phlebotomist at the practice. 'Yes.' She nodded.

'I've said I'll bring in a cake, but I'm not that great at baking and I only have a packet mix. Got any advice?'

Stacey laughed. 'Just add water, I think.'

Shelby's work friends were going to fit a small celebration for their work colleague during the lunch hour, when the surgery was closed. Pieces of paper with a selection of various food items written on them had been put into a hat and they'd each had to pull out one, telling them what they had to bring in. Stacey had got crisps and cheesy nibbles, packets of which were already in her cupboard. But she felt for Daniel, having drawn the duty of the cake. That was important— and was it fair to bring in a packet mix cake?

'I can help you,' she offered. 'You know… in the spirit of friendship. Because friends is what we are.' She smiled winningly.

Daniel nodded. 'You'd do that?'

She shrugged. 'Sure! Why not? Like you say, we're both adults. And it's just making a cake. It's not like we're getting engaged or anything.'

Daniel smiled and it warmed her heart. She liked making him smile. Liked to see the creases in the corners of his eyes, the way his eyes would light up.

'Well, I'd appreciate that. Thank you. Do

you want to come over to mine, or should I come to yours?'

'I'll come to yours. Let me tell Gran and ask her to babysit Jack. Shall I come round at about eight? Is that okay?'

'Sure.'

'I'll bring what we'll need.'

Just after eight she stood at the French doors, holding a small bag, and she smiled as he let her in.

He'd changed his shirt, she noticed, and his hair was damp. Had he had a shower since seeing her? He certainly smelt good! A dazzling array of beautiful aromas was assailing her senses. Soap. Bodywash. Shampoo. Shaving balm? All wrapped up in the stunningly handsome parcel that was Dr Daniel Prior.

She swallowed, sensing suddenly that maybe this wasn't a great idea. But she'd promised to help, so she told herself to just soldier on. She had complete control of her body and she didn't have to do anything that would complicate matters.

They were friends.

Friends.

And friends were allowed to notice if someone had made an effort to smell nice. Friends were allowed to notice if another friend looked nice.

'So, what's in the bag?' he asked.

'Lots of cake-making goodies. What have *you* got?'

Daniel smiled. 'I had a good rummage in my cupboards. I found eggs, flour, some vanilla essence that's amazingly still in date—though how I come to have it, I can't remember—and some icing sugar.'

'Perfect! Come on, then! I've found a recipe I think we ought to try.'

She put her bag down on the counter and then picked up the recipe she'd printed off the internet earlier and showed it to him.

Daniel raised an eyebrow. 'That's...ambitious. A rainbow cake? Have you ever made one of those before?'

'Yes, I have. Let's amaze our work colleagues, shall we?'

They both washed their hands at the sink, drying them off on towels. Then Stacey set Daniel to work, weighing out ingredients, as she got out bowls and cake trays and the batch of food colourings she already had.

'You're sure about this? Can we really do six tiers?' Daniel asked.

'Of course we can? You afraid?' She smiled.

'A little.'

She laughed. 'We'll be fine.'

'Okay… Caster sugar, eggs, flour, milk—all in. Where's that vanilla extract?'

'Just here.' Stacey handed it to him as if she was passing him a scalpel and he was performing surgery.

He smiled at her and added a few drops.

'Mixer.'

She passed him the electric handheld mixer and he placed it in the mix and turned it on.

'Is your gran okay staying with Jack?'

'Yes. She's happy to wait for me to get back. He'll be fine.'

When he'd finished, she helped him pour the mixture into three bowls and then started playing alchemist, adding red, orange and yellow food colouring to each of and mixing well.

'This is fun!' Daniel said. 'Much better than

me trying to half-ass my way through making a boring sponge and burning it.'

'You don't bake very often?'

'No. Not really. Penny always used to bake, though. She enjoyed it. She was always producing stuff for the village fete's bake sale.'

'Maybe we should do something for that, too, then? Join forces? Combine and conquer? I quite fancy winning a rosette.' She smiled as she added a little more yellow to the mix.

'You don't think it'll get tongues wagging if we enter a joint cake?'

'I live in your back garden. I work with you. We're both single. If you haven't realised that tongues are already wagging then there's no hope for you.'

He laughed. 'You're right.'

'Okay, let's get these three in the oven and make up another batch of mixture for the green, blue and purple layers.'

When all the cakes had been cooked, and were out cooling on racks, they began to make the icing, mixing sugar, cream cheese and butter until they had a nice thick consistency.

'We can layer them now?' asked Daniel.

'First we need to check the cakes are cool enough. If they're still hot, the icing mix will melt and we'll end up with a collapsed cake.'

'Okay. You're the boss.'

She smiled at him. 'In this kitchen, maybe.'

Stacey held the layers as Daniel began to ice them and stick them together. They worked well, laughing and giggling every time icing got smeared across their hands and fingertips. It was a messy business.

'Now I understand why I'm a doctor and not a plasterer,' he said.

'Interior decorators across the land are grateful.'

He turned and smiled at her, laughing. 'Just hold that bit still.'

They were close. Her arms almost entwined with his as he tried to get at all the curves of the cake. It was exciting being this close to him and she was enjoying it. They were involved in their task and had a focus, so being close was so much easier.

As the cake grew taller with each layer it became messier and more funny, and by the time they'd finished icing the cake they were both laughing so hard at how much mess they'd made, they'd completely forgotten their awkwardness of earlier.

Stacey put the cake in the fridge and turned to survey the mess. 'Better get this place cleaned up, I suppose… I'd hate the landlord to think I didn't clean up after myself.'

'Let me help you.'

Within ten minutes the kitchen was clean again, and all the dishes and bowls were in the dishwasher.

Stacey finished wiping down a countertop, happy that it was all done.

She turned to look at Daniel. 'All done!'

'You've missed a bit.'

'Where?' she looked around, not seeing anything.

Daniel took a step forward and she turned back and met his gaze. And that was when she realised he was concentrating hard on her face.

'You have a bit of flour just here,' he said softly, raising his hand to touch the smear she had on her chin. He held her face gently and, using his thumb, gently wiped it off. His concentration was intense. So much so, she almost couldn't breathe.

He was standing so close...gazing down at her mouth, her lips, his thumb slowly stroking her skin, every brush a scintillating delight.

She looked up at his eyes and knew in that moment she was helpless before him. She wanted this man. She had been fighting her instincts over him since the first moment she'd seen him run into The Buttered Bun. She'd known then that he was a danger. A threat to her equilibrium. And yet here she stood in his kitchen. Having just made a birthday cake with him. Having just laughed and flirted her way through an hour with him.

And now? Now he was close, smelling delicious, looking intense and broody and dark-eyed. And by God she wanted to see if he tasted as good as he looked!

But maybe he didn't want to make a move? They'd almost kissed before and look at what had happened. Maybe he didn't want that awkwardness again—because why would he? Maybe he was waiting for her permission before he made a move?

So, with her heart pounding, with her blood racing hot and needy through her veins, she reached up to him, resting her hands upon his chest, going onto tiptoe, and brought her lips to his.

It had been so long since she'd last kissed someone! Since she'd last been made to feel she was someone special. That she was important and someone other than a mother or a doctor. That she was a woman. A woman with needs and desires.

Daniel saw her. She knew he did. And the feel of his mouth upon hers was sending fireworks up into the sky between the two of them. Her nerve-endings were alight with need. Her body was pressing against the long, solid length of him. Now his hands were in her hair and he made a soft growling noise in the back of his throat… And, oh, that made her want him even more!

He pushed her back against the kitchen counter and she moaned with pleasure as his hands began to roam her body. Everywhere he touched lit up like a beacon, and then suddenly he was lifting her onto the counter and she was wrapping her legs around him, urging him closer.

It was as if time had slowed. As if the rest

of the world had fallen away to nothing and all that existed was her and Daniel.

She felt him. Tasted him. Consumed him.

All she could think of in those moments was *him*.

Blood pounding. Heart thumping. Breath racing.

She was hungry for him after starving herself of his attention for so long. After being so close to him for so long, but not being allowed to touch. To enjoy. To explore.

Now she could.

Stacey moaned in delight as his hands moved over her body, as his tongue danced with hers, and she plummeted into a world of longing and desire.

It had been so long since she'd been with anyone. There'd been no one since she'd had Jack. One or two dates, but nothing had ever come of them. She'd been too afraid to allow anything to get that far. It had been dinners. Drinks. Maybe a peck on the cheek at the end of the date. Perhaps a quick kiss on the lips, if she'd really liked them. But she'd never let it get any further. She'd kept putting on the brakes. Telling them *It's me, not you* and letting them down gently. Her world had been turned upside down by the failure of a romantic relationship and she'd been so terrified of taking anything further.

But with Daniel…

She reached for his belt, struggling with the buckle, getting frustrated, laughing when Daniel had to help her. Their lips met again as she unzipped him and took him in her hand, thrilling at his low growl. And then he was reaching up beneath her skirt to remove her underwear, pulling it off in one swift move and pulling her towards him. And when he thrust himself into her she gasped aloud and clutched him tight, allowed herself to fall completely under his spell.

When had sex ever felt like this? This need to consume, to devour, to take everything a man had to offer?

Her breathing quickened. She arched against him, felt his lips at her throat, his hot breath on her neck as he nibbled and sucked and licked, and then his lips met hers once again. He breathed her name and it was the sexiest thing she had ever heard.

A small voice in the back of her head questioned what she was doing… If this was right… If this was sensible… But she quashed it in an instant because she really didn't want to hear it. It was nonsense. Of course it was right. How could something that felt so good, be wrong?

It was only afterwards, when he'd made her come spectacularly and reached his own climax, that she stilled and gathered her breath, and her senses and the little voice got louder.

She was still entangled in him, but her brain was clearing, sense and reality beginning to intrude.

And she was terrified of what she was thinking.

There was an awkward dressing moment. Almost as if neither of them could believe what they had done.

Daniel helped her find her underwear and helped her slide it back on in a gentlemanly manner, his fingertips grazing her calves and then her thighs, until his hands were on her hips and he was gazing into her eyes again.

Even now—because it was him—she felt that she could throw caution to the wind and go for it all over again. But her mind was not so completely overcome by lust, and she remembered that her gran was waiting for her to get back to the annexe.

'I'd better go. Gran's expecting me.'

He grazed her lips with his and sighed, nodding. 'I know. Are we…okay?'

She nodded, straightening her clothes, running her hands through her hair, hoping to make herself look less…ravished. 'Do I look presentable?'

Daniel smiled. 'Of course. Always.'

She looked at him for a moment. 'I'll see you at work tomorrow?'

'Yes.' His eyes darkened as she walked away.

At the door, she turned, faced him. 'Don't forget to bring the cake.'

'I won't.'

She was searching his face, trying to decipher what she saw on it, and she read guilt in his eyes. Of course he'd feel that way. She was probably the first woman he'd slept with since losing his wife. At least, she hoped she was. Because now that she thought about it she realised that in their desperate need for each other they hadn't used a condom. But he didn't look the type to sleep around. What she knew of him told her the same thing. He was a decent guy. No fly-by-night. No gigolo. No player.

He was a gentleman. A gentleman who could make her heart race so fast she thought it might explode.

I'm on the pill. It should be fine.

She said goodbye and made it back to the annexe, feeling guilty, as if she'd been out on the town past her bedtime.

Her gran was waiting for her by the front door. 'Oh! Stacey! I was beginning to get worried about you. Everything okay?'

'Yep! Good. All good.'

'The cake went well?'

'Perfectly. I think Shelby will be very pleased.'

'Well, you look happy—though I'm sure that's more to do with Daniel than any baking you might have done.'

She blushed. 'Whatever do you mean?'

Her gran tilted her head to one side. 'Oh, come on. I know you like him. Don't you think I haven't noticed how you change when you talk about him?'

'I don't change! What on earth are you going on about?'

'Your voice! Your voice changes when you say his name… *Daniel*. Like he's someone special.'

'He's my landlord! And a work colleague.'

'And…?' Gran grinned.

'And nothing! Now, I've kept you later than I should have, because we had to wait for the cakes to cool, but now I'm here you can get back to Grandad. Want me to order you a taxi?'

'Your grandad is already on his way to pick me up.'

'Okay. Well, thanks for babysitting Jack.'

'My pleasure. Now, what's that in your hair…?' Gran stepped forward to reach for something.

Stacey blushed and waited, nervous to see what it was.

It was a sprinkle. One of the many that she and Daniel had sprinkled on top of the cake when they'd finished icing it.

Her gran smiled knowingly.

It seemed to take an age before her grandad arrived, and Stacey was so happy when he did. Having her gran around, smiling at her as if she knew Stacey's secret, was getting to be a bit much.

When they'd gone, Stacey locked the door with a huge sigh, thinking over the last few hours.

She'd had active, vigorous, kitchen counter sex with Daniel! She'd never done anything like that before in her entire life! With Jerry, even at the beginning, they'd always been in a bedroom, but she'd considered her sex-life quite fine, thank you very much.

But with Daniel…

Stacey opened Jack's bedroom door to check on him quietly, and saw that he was sound asleep. She closed his door and headed for her own room. She brushed her teeth in the ensuite bathroom and then headed to bed, after getting into the tee shirt and shorts that she liked to wear to sleep in.

She opened her bedside drawer to take out the contraceptive pills that she took to help with her heavy periods and realised that the days didn't match up. If this packet was right, she'd not taken a pill last night, nor the night before that!

Feeling heat rise in her cheeks, she took the pill for today and told herself she'd be fine. There was no other choice. She couldn't take the morning-after pill as she was allergic to the main ingredient, levornogestrel. She'd found that out after a condom had broken early in her relationship with Jerry. Not a pleasant few days... Symptoms-wise or Jerry-wise...

Besides, loads of people had sex all the time and didn't get pregnant. She and Daniel hadn't been careful, but technically she was on the pill and...

I'll be fine. Anything else isn't worth thinking about.

Daniel lay in bed, unable to sleep, his gaze resting on his and Penny's wedding photo. In it, they stood within the arched doorway of the church, holding hands and looking at the photographer. They were both beaming with happiness, absolutely sure that their marriage was going to be for ever. That they were going to be different. That their marriage was going to make it until they were old and grey and giving interviews to the local paper on the secret of a successful marriage.

They'd even joked about it once. He'd told Penny how much he loved her and how, in the future, he'd tell anyone willing to listen that the secret to a good marriage was to be loyal and honest, no matter what. And he'd truly believed that. Loyalty and honesty mattered the most to him, and even after that drunk driver had run them off the road he'd believed he would always be loyal to his wife. Even after her death.

But it appeared that wasn't true at all.

And Daniel was struggling with that.

He'd never imagined himself with anyone else. He really hadn't. And then Stacey had come into his life. Working with him. Living in his annexe. And she was perfect and beautiful and, God damn it, she'd got under his skin!

And tonight... Neither of them had planned that. It had been unexpected and surprising and off-the-charts scorching hot! His senses, his logic—all had gone out of the window just from touching her and tasting her. He'd fought his attraction to her for so long... To finally be able to indulge himself in how she felt and tasted, how she moaned and gasped and hungered for him in turn, had been...

There were no words.

But all he could think about now was that he'd been with another woman. Something he'd never imagined when he'd wed Penny. They should have been together for ever, but death had parted them. She and Mason had been taken too soon and he'd been left behind. Unable to help them. Unable to protect them. And surely because of that he didn't deserve to find happiness with anyone else? Doing so would be a betrayal of his promise to his wife.

But did it matter that he'd broken his promise? Who knew about it, after all, except for himself and Stacey? Others might be thrilled for him to find happiness with someone else. Genevieve and William would be, that was for sure.

We didn't use protection.

In the heat of the moment he just hadn't thought. What he had been doing with Stacey had just felt so right, so normal, so *nec-*

essary, that his brain hadn't been telling him to remember to take precautions!

I'll check with her in the morning. See if she's on the pill, or something.

They were both doctors. They'd be sensible about this. As much as they could be *after* the act...

Rolling over, he turned away from the photo and stared up at the ceiling.

So far that morning Stacey had treated a case of postnatal depression, a fungal toenail, dealt with a referral request for a knee issue and a case of scarlet fever. There was a knock at her door and Daniel slipped in.

Instantly, she blushed, then smiled, standing to greet him. 'Good morning.'

He came to her. Stopped. Seemed unsure as to how to greet her, then decided on a brief kiss on her cheek.

'Good morning. How are you today?'

She nodded. 'I'm good. You?'

'I'm fine.'

'Good.'

Having him in the room with her, standing

this close, it was as if her fingers were inching forward to entwine with his…

'I…er…thought that after last night I ought to check that we're…covered.'

Was he blushing? She liked it that he was. It was endearing.

'I'm on the pill, if that's what you were asking?'

He gave a brief embarrassed laugh. 'Yeah. I was. Phew! Okay…'

Should she tell him that she'd missed a couple of tablets? What would that garner but his stress to deal with alongside her own? There was no point in stressing him out. Not unless there was something to stress about, anyway.

'I haven't been with anyone since my wife,' he said. 'So you don't have to worry about STDs.'

'That's good to know. And I've only ever been with Jerry, so…'

He nodded. Seemed happy with her answer, too. It was a minefield these days… STDs were on the rise, especially among younger people. Diseases like gonorrhoea and chlamydia were not worried about as much as they used to be because there were medications available to treat them.

It was not something she wanted to consider.

'I don't think either of us needs the complication of an unexpected pregnancy or an uncomfortable visitor,' he said.

'No! Absolutely not!' she agreed, smiling as he pressed his forehead against hers.

He looked deeply into her eyes and then, in an instant, they were kissing again.

Heat rose in her body as she reawakened to his touch and attention. Every touch, every stroke, every caress of his hands made her come alive. And the fact that they were doing this at work… In secret… As if it was forbidden… Made it even better!

She'd lain in bed last night, telling herself not to be so stupid as to think that it meant something. It was a fling—that was all. She couldn't stop herself when she was with Daniel. It was impossible! She was drawn to him like a moth to a flame. Like a bee to a flower. Like a sunflower to the sun. She had to go to him. Turn to him. Embrace him. It was as if she couldn't get enough of him.

It was only the knock on her door that made them suddenly break apart, guiltily and breathlessly, creating space between them. Stacey sat down behind her desk and Daniel stood on the opposite side, as if he'd just popped in for a chat.

'Come in?' she said.

It was Hannah, the advanced nurse practitioner. 'Oh, hi. Sorry… Am I interrupting?'

'No! Not at all!' Stacey hoped she wasn't blushing. 'How can I help?'

'I've got a patient who's come in with a rash on her chest, and I can feel a lump. Would you come and check it out for me?'

Stacey looked at her morning list. Her next patient hadn't arrived yet, so she had time. 'Sure!'

Daniel smiled. 'I'll catch you later? At lunch?'

Stacey nodded. 'You will.'

Shelby's birthday party went brilliantly. She'd clearly had no idea that the other staff had planned a celebration for her, and she cried some happy tears, when she saw the spread they'd put on for her.

'And that cake! Who made that? Was it you, Gayle?' Shelby asked one of the ladies on Reception, who was renowned for making cakes and bringing them in as treats for everyone.

'No, not me.'

'Then who?'

Daniel raised his hand. 'I made it. With help from Stacey.'

Shelby looked happily surprised. 'Who knew you had this in you?'

Daniel was pleased to have put a smile on Shelby's face. He glanced at Stacey and gave her a wink, before looking over at Zach, who had caught him winking.

Zach smiled knowingly and raised an eyebrow at Daniel.

He turned away from his friend's knowing look and passed Shelby the cake knife, leading the group in a rousing chorus of 'Happy Birthday'.

When it was over, she cut into the tower of cake and squealed. 'A rainbow cake! Oh, my God, this is awesome!' Shelby threw her arms around Daniel and gave him a huge hug, before turning and hugging Stacey. 'You two are awesome!'

Stacey smiled.

Daniel was feeling great. He'd missed this. He'd not realised how much he'd withdrawn from everyone over the last couple of years. It was as if his pain and grief had isolated him from everyone—but not because they'd turned away from him. They'd tried to help. He was the one who had kept everyone at arm's length.

Before, when there'd been birthday parties at work, or other celebrations, he'd given muted congratulations, raised his mug in a toast and then slipped quietly back into his consulting room to be by himself. Seeing others so happy when he still hurt had been overwhelming. He hadn't hated it that they were happy. It had just been that their happiness made him sad, because he'd known he'd never be happy again.

And then he'd made a connection. Allowed himself to get close to Stacey and Jack. And by doing so he'd started doing other small things that were reintegrating him into society. He'd made a cake for a work colleague. Done it with Stacey. And seeing the joy of something he'd done showing on Shelby's face in absolute delight... Well, that made him feel wonderful.

To begin with he had felt as if Stacey was a wrecking ball. Breaking down his carefully constructed walls while he kept trying to rapidly rebuild them and protect himself. But he couldn't protect himself from her, and that was what made being with her so terrifying and exciting all at the same time. Being with her had brought him back to life again, making him feel he could partake in other people's happiness again—because *he* was happy again.

All because of her.

And then there was Jack... Dear, wonderful Jack. A little boy who'd been through his own trauma and had begun to heal here.

He'd like to think he'd had a hand in that. That in some way he'd helped Jack feel he had another friend. He'd played football with him, fixed things with him, taught him to use a hammer. They'd gardened together, read stories together, and most of all they'd *talked*. And laughed. And enjoyed each other's company. Something Daniel himself had never thought he'd be able to do.

Yes, he felt guilty, but that was natural after all he'd been through. It didn't mean he didn't love Penny. Or that he would forget her and Mason. How could he? That could never happen.

But maybe now he was beginning to accept that perhaps he didn't have to be alone for the rest of his life?

He looked at Stacey across the room, chatting with Hannah. She was a beautiful person, inside and out. He was so glad he'd let out his annexe to her and Jack. He had been emboldened by doing so and it made his life better. All because of them.

He went to stand by her. 'The cake's a hit. Thank you very much.'

She gave him a secret nudge with her arm. 'You're very welcome.'

Shelby was handing out slices of cake to everyone and Daniel had to admit it did look great. All those colours! It was perfect. And he would never have managed it without Stacey. Without her, there might be a questionable Victoria Sponge sitting on the counter instead, most likely with burnt edges hidden under icing sugar. But because of what he and Stacey had created everyone was so happy. So delighted. And he liked the feeling it engendered in him.

Maybe *everything* that he and Stacey did together would bring happiness?

'Only a couple more weeks until the village fete,' said Gran, as she and Stacey sat together at her grandparents' kitchen table having a cup of tea together the next weekend.

'I know! Are you entering any of the competitions?' Stacey asked.

'I've got a plum and ginger jam I might enter. And I know your grandad is going to enter one of his giant marrows. He came second place last year—do you remember me telling you?'

'I remember the newspaper cutting you sent, yes.'

Outside in the back garden Jack was playing football with Daniel on the lawn.

'Those two get along brilliantly, don't they?' said Gran, conversationally.

Stacey watched them. Jack was grinning—

beaming—playing happily with Daniel, who at that moment in time was trying to dribble the ball past Jack to get towards the goal.

'They do. It's nice to see him so happy.'

'Do you mean Jack? Or Daniel?'

Stacey turned to look at her gran, who had one of those weird, happy but knowing looks on her face. 'What do you mean?'

'Oh, come now… I've told you before. It's perfectly obvious to me that you and Daniel have very strong feelings for one another.'

Stacey shook her head, laughing, and turned away. 'Don't be silly. We're just friends.'

'Don't think I haven't noticed how he looks at you. How he likes to stand close to you. How you touch each other when you think no one's looking.'

'Gran!'

Her gran smiled. 'It's *lovely*, darling. That poor man has been through hell in the last few years, and to see him smile the way you make him smile… That warms my heart… it really does. He deserves happiness and so do you. You've both been through the mill.'

Stacey wanted to protest, but what was

the point? Gran saw everything. Maybe she ought to set herself up at the village fete with a crystal ball?

'I do like him, yes, but I've got to be cautious, too.'

'Because of Jack?'

She nodded.

'Daniel loves Jack. Look at them together. It's good for him to be around my great-grandson. It brings him to life again. I understand your caution, but don't let it hold you back, dear. Knowing Daniel, no matter what happened between the two of you, that man would be there for your boy for ever.'

'You think so?' Stacey asked wistfully, watching the two of them once again.

Gran was right. They *were* good together. But Stacey had had her life ruined once before by a romantic relationship in the workplace going wrong. She wouldn't be able to bear it if it happened again and she lost everything. Because she was the interloper here. Even though she'd grown up in Greenbeck, she'd left. Daniel had been here for years. This place felt like his. Her work colleagues were his. Her friends were his. If something were to go wrong, would she lose everything all over again and be forced to move away?

I couldn't. Jack is happy at school and his happiness has to come first.

'I do,' said her gran. 'He's an honourable man.'

Yes, she thought. *He is.*

Daniel was nothing like Jerry. If something bad were to happen between them she couldn't imagine Daniel trying to drive her out of the practice, the way Jerry had. And besides, she was sick of running. Greenbeck was where she wanted to start putting down roots.

Outside, Jack scored a goal and came running back towards Daniel, arms in the air, yelling with delight. Daniel gave him a high five, then whirled her son around in the air, celebrating with him.

She smiled. Seeing them together made her happy.

After their football, Jack and Daniel lay back on the grass, breathing heavily and staring at the white clouds drifting by overhead.

'That one looks like a dog,' Jack said, pointing.

'It does! A little terrier. What about that one?' It was Daniel's turn to point.

'A kite?'

'Yep! You know, I made a kite once...'

Jack turned to look at him. 'You *made* one? How did you do that? Could you teach me?'

'Sure! I got taught at my Scout group when I was your age.'

'What else do they do at Scouts?'

'Well...lots of things. They all work together and have fun earning different badges. First aid, cooking, sewing, woodwork, metalwork... Anything you can imagine. It's fun!'

'I like the sound of that.'

'Well, there's a local Beaver Scouts group here in Greenbeck. Maybe you should ask your mum about it?'

'I'm not sure...'

'Are you worried about the other children?' he asked gently.

'A bit.'

'Believe you me, there's no bullying in Scouts. Everyone works together. The leaders work hard to create an atmosphere that is friendly and kind, and everyone looks out for one another. You're a group. A team. I think it'd be great for building up your confidence.'

'You think so?'

'I do! You've already made such huge strides here. I really think you could take on the world if you wanted! Do anything!'

Jack smiled, and Daniel liked seeing him do so. He truly was building his confidence and growing his friendship groups at school. Being involved in the Scouts could surely only help that.

'Want me to talk to your mum about it?' he asked.

Jack nodded.

'Okay. Ready for the second half?' He grabbed the football.

Jack laughed and got to his feet.

They all walked home together. It was a nice cool evening and perfect for a stroll. Jack was ahead of them, bouncing his football as he walked.

'You've done such a lot for Jack,' Stacey said. 'Being his friend…'

He smiled. 'Well, he's helped me, too.'

'He has?'

'Of course. Being around a kid his age again… I wasn't sure I'd be able to handle it, to tell you the truth.'

'Because of your son?'

He nodded, his eyes darkening.

'You must miss him terribly.'

'I do. Sometimes so much it hurts. And then I feel guilty, because being with you two makes me smile. And sometimes when I'm with you I forget about the heartache and the pain, but when you're gone again I remember and feel worse.'

She nodded in understanding. 'Life's a roller coaster. It's fine when you're on a high, but there are always those drops, reminding you that there's a long way to fall if you're not careful.'

'Are *we* being careful, do you think?'

'How do you mean?'

'In what we're doing? Are we taking a risk in thinking we can be happy?'

'We *are* happy, aren't we? When we're together?'

Daniel nodded in assent. 'We are. I know we are. But I also know I'm waiting for that fall you mentioned. Relationships are tough, and the longer you're in one, the more complications arrive.'

'Are you saying you want to take a step back?'

He stopped walking, turned to look at her. 'No. Most definitely not. Are you?'

She smiled. 'No.'

They began walking again, watching Jack up ahead, keeping an eye on him.

'I guess I'm saying I just don't want to get hurt. And I don't want to hurt either of you two.'

'Ditto. So, let's make a pact, then. If there's an issue we talk to one another about it. We don't brood. We don't fret. We're open with one another. We face it. Talk it through like adults.'

Daniel nodded. 'Sounds good to me.'

'Shake on it?' She held out her hand.

He laughed and shook it.

Jack had been in bed for ages and Daniel was watching the end of a movie with Stacey. They were sitting together on the couch, and halfway through Daniel had reached out for her hand and taken it in his.

It had felt right, and the entire time he'd been sitting there, next to her, he'd wanted to hold her.

The movie was an action-adventure film, and although it was good, it wasn't as wonderful as it was just to sit there and be holding Stacey's hand, feeling as if he was part of something special. Something new and exciting and vibrant.

When the credits rolled, she laid her head upon his shoulder and relaxed into him.

He savoured the moment, closing his eyes and just enjoying it. Eventually she lifted her head and turned to look at him. Her green eyes bright and shining, she asked, 'Do you want to stay over?'

He did. Very much so.

'What about Jack?'

'If you leave before he wakes in the morning he'll never know.' she said enticingly, reaching up to pull his lips towards hers.

The kiss was electric. Even more so than it had been before. Full of promise and secrets and delights.

He pulled back for a breath, switched off the TV with the remote and then stood, leading her towards her bedroom, closing the bedroom door softly behind them.

For a moment he just looked at her. Taking her in. Those tumbles of red hair, dark in the shadows. Her green eyes, looking up at him with so much want and anticipation. Suddenly he couldn't wait a moment longer and he was in her arms. Stumbling towards the bed. Falling backwards so that she lay atop him. Pulling her close, deepening the kiss, struggling to remove clothes and feel the heat of skin and intimate connection.

Barriers removed, he rolled her over onto her back and pinned her arms above her head as his lips went to her throat. She gasped, arching up to meet him, whispering his name.

He couldn't deny the heat between them. It was as if they were made for each other. The fire in his belly burned for her. The scorching furnace of his blood raged in its intensity to light up every single nerve-ending in his body. And where they connected, skin to skin, he imagined sparks of electricity between them.

He needed her so much! Had yearned for her so much these last couple of days, wondering if they'd get to be together again. Something so right could never be wrong.

Stacey was perfect, and even though he yearned to be within her he held off for as long as he could. Waiting. Teasing. Delighting in watching her urge him on.

They were as quiet as they could be, but her gasps and heavy breathing were enough, and finally, when he could wait no longer, he slid into her and thrust long, hard and slow. He watched her face, kissing her, building his pace, until she erupted beneath him and he rode her wave with his own.

His lips returned to hers. A kiss. A breath. Another kiss. It was as if he didn't want to let her go. Didn't want to be not touching her. But he rolled to her side and pulled her close, smiling with satisfaction as she cuddled into him. She draped her leg over his and let out a delicious sigh.

They didn't need to say anything.

Their bodies had said everything they needed to say to each other.

And once he was sure she was asleep he closed his eyes and drifted off into a dream-world of his own.

Each night after that Daniel shared her bed, getting up at around six a.m. to creep from the annexe and return to his own home.

Those moments were agony for Stacey. Their nights were steamy, their dreams dreamy, but when her gentle alarm woke them in the early hours they had to leave the little fantasy world they'd built and part, returning to reality.

Daniel would groan at having to leave her bed, and sometimes, unable to bear him going, she would grab him and pull him back onto the bed, kiss him and hold him and stroke him in places that she knew would drive him wild.

But always he would stop her and tell her, 'I have to go. Jack will be awake soon.'

And then she'd let him go.

They were doing the right thing. Of course they were. She didn't want to give Jack any hopes about Daniel being a permanent fixture in their lives. It was bad enough as it was. Jack *adored* Daniel. They played football and badminton together all the time. Daniel made time for her son and she loved that. But sometimes she worried about what she was doing.

What if it all went wrong?

She couldn't help but be fatalistic. Every other relationship she'd had had gone bad. Why would this one be any different?

Only it *felt* different. She couldn't understand why, but did that difference mean that she could depend on it going well? She didn't know, and so she was scared all the time. Waiting for the ball to drop. Waiting for something awful to go wrong and ruin everything.

Sometimes Daniel caught her having those dark moments.

'What's wrong?' he'd ask.

'I'm waiting for the bubble to burst.'

And he'd kiss her forehead, or her cheeks, or her lips, and stroke her face and comfort her.

'I don't know what the future holds for us. Let's just try to enjoy what we have right now.'

And she'd smile back and kiss him back, because he was right. If she spent all her time worrying about the future she'd never enjoy the present. And these rare moments of happiness were too good to miss or not appreciate. He was her special secret right now. And it was amazing.

For too long she'd been so stressed and worried about Jack. About how to make his life better. Moving all the way down the country in the hopes of finding a new life. In a place where they could both thrive. Daniel was making her feel that right now she could. That joy and contentment were possible for her. And that was too valuable for her to throw away.

As she drove into work one morning, she began to see preparations for the village fete. Bunting was being hung up all over the place—all around the village green, in front of the shops and the pub, and even at the surgery. People were working hard on making their gardens look nice, and flowers were in abundance everywhere she looked. Pink and purple. Roses and clematis. Hollyhocks, foxgloves and lupins. All standing proud and pretty.

And everyone seemed to have a smile.

Her first patient was coming in for a coil insertion—a young woman who'd had her second baby just over two months ago.

Phoebe Harrow entered the room with her baby asleep in a pushchair. 'Sorry. I couldn't get anyone to watch him. But he should sleep for another hour anyway.'

Stacey smiled. 'It's no problem.'

She went over with Phoebe the procedure that would take place, what to expect, and how to check that the intrauterine device was still in place afterwards. She described the side effects she might notice and told her how to deal with any discomfort or bleeding afterwards.

When Phoebe was happy with everything, Stacey sent a screen message through to Rachel, their HCA, to say that they were ready.

Rachel wheeled a small trolley through, draped with blue paper to protect the sterile field, and positioned it next to the examination bed after Phoebe lay down.

Stacey opened up Phoebe's vagina to take a

good look at the cervix, and nodded to Rachel to unseal the packet that contained the IUD.

'Okay, nice steady breaths and try to relax.'

The IUD went in smoothly, which Stacey was glad of—and no doubt Phoebe too. There was a minimum amount of blood. When Rachel had left the room, Stacey taught her patient how to feel for the IUD and check that it was still in place.

'All good?'

'Perfect! Thank God that's over! I thought it would be much more painful than that. Now I can relax a little bit. I love my kids...but I don't want any more!' she said, and laughed as she stood to get dressed.

Stacey smiled as she removed her gloves and washed her hands in the small sink. 'Two can be a handful. How old is your other one?'

'Seven. Quite a gap, I know. Just as I got my life back—bingo! I was pregnant again. My surprise baby. But...' she pulled back the curtain and emerged from behind it, smiling at her baby '...he's so perfect I can't imagine life without him. Isn't that odd? Because I was terrified when I found out I was expecting again.'

'It must have been quite a surprise if you weren't trying.'

She shook her head. 'We weren't. And we were using protection. But sometimes those suckers just get through no matter what, huh?' She laughed again, and gently rocked the pushchair as her little one snuffled a bit.

Stacey nodded. 'What's meant to be will be. Now, remember—you can take paracetamol if you need it. Any cramps or bleeding should soon stop, but you can always call us if you think there's an issue. I'll book you in for a check-up in about…four weeks? Just to make sure it's still in place and you're not having any problems.'

Phoebe nodded. 'Sounds great!'

Stacey went through the calendar on the computer and brought up her appointments for those days, finding an empty spot just before lunchtime.

'Does that date work for you?'

'Yes.'

She waved Phoebe and her surprise baby away and began to type up her notes. She was glad the insertion had gone smoothly, because she was starting to feel a little bit of a headache. Bending over and twisting at weird angles to insert the coil certainly hadn't helped! She felt better sitting back at her desk, but she opened a drawer, found her own packet of paracetamol and took a couple, just to stave off anything worse. She felt peckish, too, so whilst she had a couple of minutes she ate half the ham salad sandwich that she'd picked up earlier.

She'd eat the rest outside and enjoy a bit of sunshine at lunchtime...

Daniel saw her sitting outside on a bench by the village green. She sat there, eyes closed, face turned upwards to the sun, just enjoying the warmth and the beautiful day. For a brief moment he stood and looked at her, realising how much he felt for her.

He loved to see her happy and content.

He loved spending time with her and Jack.

And he wanted to spend more.

So, smiling, he crossed the road, holding up his hand to thank the driver who let him skip across the road, and walked across the verdant green grass to settle himself down on the bench next to her.

She opened her eyes and smiled when she saw it was him.

'Hey,' he said.

'Hey…'

'You looked so perfectly relaxed. I had to join you.'

'Why not? It's gorgeous here. Feel that sun… I missed that in Scotland. Don't get me wrong. Sometimes we had the most beautiful days. Just not that many. And when I popped out for lunch there wasn't a park or a green near the surgery, so I'd drag a chair outside and sit in the car park.'

He smiled. 'It's not the same, is it?'

She laughed. 'No. It's not.'

She blinked and watched him open up his packed lunch. A delicious aroma emerged.

'What have you got there?' she asked.

'Coronation chicken. Want one?'

'Ooh, yes, please!' She sat up straighter and he proffered her half the sandwich, which she devoured in seconds.

'Wow? Did you not pack yourself any lunch?'

'I did, but I ate most of it earlier. I was starving.'

'Long morning?'

'No. Perfectly ordinary. I was just hungry.'

He smiled. It got that way sometimes. 'Is it okay to come round again later?'

'Sure! I could do us some dinner. What do you fancy?'

'Anything is great. But I do have an ulterior motive.'

She raised an eyebrow. 'If it's to take advantage of my body again, I may just let you!'

He smiled. 'Understood. Actually, I wanted to talk to you about Jack.'

Her smile disappeared. 'Why? What's wrong?'

'Nothing's wrong. It's just we were talking the other day about him being a Beaver Scout. I told him I used to be one and he seemed interested. He asked me to talk to you about it.'

'He asked *you*? He didn't feel he could tell me himself?'

He could see she was hurt by this. 'He's getting on great at school, and he heard my stories about camping and activities with the Beavers and he wanted to give it a try. I said I'd ask you if I could take him. They do introductory visits. You don't have to pay for the first couple...just see if he likes it or not.'

'Oh.' She stared out across the grass towards the duckpond. 'I should be glad. I know he's happy. Why do I feel like he's suddenly growing up?'

'Because you've been his rock all this time. He's only ever needed you. Now he's spreading his wings, as all little boys do.'

She nodded, forcing a brave smile. 'Okay. You can take him. Or maybe we should take him together?'

Now it was his turn to feel surprised. 'You're happy to do that?'

'Yes.'

'Okay. Let's do it.'

CHAPTER EIGHT

STACEY WAS SO incredibly nervous that her stomach actually felt queasy! She couldn't remember the last time she'd been so nervous!

Actually, I can. Jack's first day at Greenbeck Juniors and my first day at the surgery.

She would be leaving him. Letting him walk away and knowing he was in someone else's hands. She had trusted that the school would protect him, and now that trust would be placed with the Beavers leaders and all the other children.

Most she recognised from Jack's school, so hopefully that was a good sign. There were kids here that he already knew.

They were meeting in the Scout hut, which was situated down the road from the church. At the back of the hut was a long row of wooden benches. Stacey and Daniel sat there and watched.

She felt anxiety building in her throat as

her son stood alone, not sure what he ought to be doing. Her desire to go to him was strong, but just as she was about to get up out of her seat and go and take his hand, tell him they could go home, his friend Sam saw him and pulled him into the throng. She heard a chorus of cheers at his arrival.

'See? Nothing to worry about,' said Daniel.

She smiled at him. 'I can't help it.'

He placed his hand on hers reassuringly. 'I can see that. Try to picture yourself sunning yourself on that bench again, as you were the other day. Pretend that you're not actually in a small hall filled with loud children armed with whistles.'

She nodded, looking for Jack again. She saw him instantly. The only one not in a blue Beavers polo shirt. Seeing him involved and happy should be making her feel better, but her stomach was still churning slightly.

Wow! I really have got myself worked up.

She searched in her handbag and found an old packet of mints. She sucked on one and hoped it would help.

I'm probably just hungry, too.

It had been a long day and she was still yet to cook.

Stacey had wanted to impress Daniel with her culinary prowess and create a meal that would leave him asking for seconds and thirds, but at this rate they'd be calling into the chippy on the way home and getting something fast. She wasn't sure she had the patience, or enough mints, to hold off the hunger and the nausea.

It was a long hour and a half, but Jack had a whale of a time, and afterwards he bounced over towards Stacey and Daniel and asked if he could join straight away?

'We'll do it next week. I promise. Come on—you must be starving!'

Jack nodded, and skipped ahead to find the car.

'See? Nothing to worry about,' said Daniel, his hand in the small of her back as he followed her out, being careful not to let Jack see him touching her.

She was grateful that he was sensitive to that.

They got into the car and Jack babbled non-stop all the way to the chip shop and all the way home. The smell of fish and chips with salt and vinegar permeated the car, and Stacey was practically salivating by the time they made it inside and served up.

'Let's eat in the garden,' suggested Daniel.

So they made their way to his patio and sat down on his outdoor chairs and began to eat.

The food was delicious and really hit the spot! Soft, fluffy chips and meaty, thick fish in crunchy batter. She hadn't been sure she'd eat it all, but she did—very quickly—and washed it down with some orange juice that Daniel had prepared earlier and left in his fridge.

'Are you looking forward to the village fete?' he asked.

'I am! I haven't been to one since I left the village, but I have fond memories of them. I'm sure Jack will like them too, now that his confidence has grown and he's got some friends.'

'And the baby-judging?'

She groaned. 'Hmm… I'm not so sure. I didn't ask to do it—Gran volunteered me. But how do you judge *babies*? Aren't we supposed to say they're all wonderful? How do we go about picking a winner?'

Daniel shrugged. 'I don't know... Judge the outfit and not the child?'

'But even so...' She really didn't like the idea of it at all, and just the thought of it made her feel incredibly uncomfortable. 'And what about the parents? They're the ones with all the hopes! They're the ones thinking that their child is adorable and bound to win. And when they don't... I hope we don't get hated!'

'I'm sure we won't. Everyone knows it's just a bit of fun.'

She must still look ill at ease. Fidgety, maybe. Because Daniel asked, 'Want to go for a walk?'

She looked at him and nodded.

They set off into the village, taking with them a bag of peas for Jack to feed the ducks and the pair of swans that had taken up residence at the pond. She and Daniel stood back, watching him, and Daniel took the moment to slip his hand into hers.

She turned to look at him and smiled.

'Are you happy?' he asked.

'I am. Are you?'

He nodded. 'I am. If you'd told me a few months ago that my whole life would change with the arrival of a new GP at the practice I would have laughed and told you not to be so ridiculous.'

'And if you'd told me I would come back home and fall for another GP at the same practice I worked at, I would have done the same!'

He smiled. 'You've fallen for me.'

The ducks had surrounded Jack, quacking and waddling. Some were floating on the water, but most had clambered onto the grass to get closer to the little boy with the food. But his throwing handful after handful of peas meant he was soon about to run out, and when he did the birds all quacked their annoyance and one even pecked at his trainer.

Jack giggled and ran back to Stacey, who had by then slipped her hand out of Daniel's.

'Come on, let's walk.'

There was a public footpath that led through the village. To the south it ran into the New Forest, and to the north, just behind the surgery, it took them up the hill towards the castle ruins. Because Jack was with them, they decided to take the north path.

What started off as a nice, meandering walk, soon turned into quite an uphill trek! But Jack seemingly hardly noticed. He ran here and there, clambering over fallen trees and investigating clumps of mushrooms, then finding himself a nice stick. Daniel seemed to be tackling it easily too, but Stacey was huffing and puffing as her leg muscles burned.

'I thought I was fitter than this!' she breathed.

'Come on, Mummy!' Jack laughed, skipping ahead to a tree with a hollow trunk and investigating.

Daniel turned back to grin at her and she made a 'time out' sign with her hands and sat down on a fallen log. 'I just need five minutes…'

She sat there, her hands on her knees, breathing heavily, quite unable to believe that a simple walk had her out of breath like this! Normally she considered herself quite fit, but actually, when was the last time she'd gone to the gym? Or the swimming pool? Or partaken in any exercise that didn't involve her being naked with Daniel?

'We'll have to get you doing a bit more cardio,' he joked.

'Looks like it. I guess this is what you get for sitting down at work all day.'

Daniel laughed and held out his hand for her to take. 'Come on. I think Jack would like to reach the castle before dark.'

She smiled ruefully and accepted his hand, and soon they were off again, heading up to Castle Merrick.

From what she remembered, the castle had stood for centuries, looking down over what had originally been a small hamlet called Greenbeck. It had grown into a village sometime around the eighteenth century.

The castle itself had been built for Lord Edwin Merrick, a man who'd had three wives, losing the first two in childbirth and outliving the third after she'd died of some sort of respiratory illness. Of his five children, four had been killed in battle and the fifth, the only girl, had entered a nunnery. So the Merrick line had ended. The castle had fallen into disrepair and was today a sight-seeing attraction, with a nearby gift shop and coffee house.

These were both now closed, due to it being so late in the evening, but the castle ruins were there for anyone to have a look around, at any time of the day or night.

Now that the uphill climb was over, Stacey's leg muscles were feeling a bit better. If only the same could be said for her body in general. She felt exhausted! The trek up the hill from the village had really done her in, and all she wanted to do was just lie down and take a nap!

But Jack was excitedly exploring the ruins, and Daniel still had her hand in his, so she allowed herself to be pulled along—even if she did keep yawning.

Daniel turned to her and grinned. 'Tired?'

'You bet. Must be all these nights you've kept me awake with your physical demands.' She smiled, stroking his face when she knew Jack wouldn't see.

'Complaining?' he asked, with mock hurt.

Stacey laughed. 'Not at all! It's one of the best ways to lose sleep, if we're going to rank reasons for a lack of it.'

'Agreed.'

He took a look around and then pulled her close. Her hips pressed to his as he took her face in his hands and moved in for a kiss.

It was illicit and exciting! And even though she knew she really ought to not be doing this, in case Jack saw them, she didn't have it in her to push him away. She wanted him. All of him! And a kiss would have to be enough.

When they broke apart, grinning at each other, they realised that Jack was standing next to them, looking up at them quizzically.

Stacey blushed and rapidly stepped away from Daniel, pasting a smile upon her face and trying to act innocent. 'Have you seen the portcullis gate, Jack?'

But Jack wasn't stupid, and he refused to be redirected. 'Are you my mummy's boyfriend?' he asked Daniel.

Daniel glanced at her. Clearly she was the one who needed to answer, but what to say? She didn't want to lie to Jack, now that he had caught them kissing like that.

'Well...erm...what would you say if he was?'

Jack just shrugged. 'I'd be fine with it.'

Stacey smiled at the nonchalant way in which he'd answered and then looked up at Daniel, who was letting out a breath of relief and smiling himself. *Wow.* That could have gone so many ways! And yet it didn't bother Jack as much as she'd thought the news of a man in her life would!

'Okay… Well, we're just seeing how it goes, all right?'

'Okay!' And he ran off to explore some more.

Stacey turned to Daniel. 'Well, that went better than I expected it would.'

'He does know me. It's not like I'm a stranger.'

'I guess… And you do spend an awful lot of time with him. I know he likes you a lot.'

'Well, that's important to me. Almost as much as it is that *you* like me a lot.'

She smiled at him. 'I do.'

'How much?'

She blushed and turned away, not really looking where she was going, not really aware of her surroundings, and tripped over a protruding rock.

Down she went, hands out to break her fall.

She felt her head connect with the ground, felt a sharp pain to the front of her face, and when she felt Daniel's arms around her, helping her into a sitting position, blood began to drip down her forehead.

'You're bleeding!' Daniel squatted down in front of her, his face full of worry and concern.

A strong ache was blooming in her head and she winced, trying to stem the blood.

Daniel reached into his pocket for his phone.

'What are you doing?' she asked.

'Ringing for an ambulance.'

'I'm fine.'

'You hit your head on a rock and now you have a cut that needs stitches. There's no way you're walking all the way back to Greenbeck. Jack? *Jack!*' he called, turning around to look for her son.

Jack came into view, smiling, then frowned when he saw his mum sitting on the ground, holding her head. His little face was a mask of shock when he saw the blood. 'What happened to Mummy?'

'She tripped and fell. But she's going to be all right—okay, champ?'

Jack nodded and sank onto the grass next to her, taking her hand in his.

She smiled at him gratefully, trying to act as if this was nothing, because she didn't want him to be worried. 'We're going to get frequent flyer miles at the hospital at this rate.'

'Some people will do anything to get out of judging a baby competition,' Daniel joked as he tore a strip from the bottom of his shirt and used it to stem the bleeding. 'Press here.'

Stacey sat with her back against some stones, feeling an utter fool. She hurt, and she was tired, and honestly all she wanted to do was go to sleep and sort out the wound in the morning.

It took some time for the ambulance to get there, and the paramedics apologised and said they were swamped at the moment. They got them all into the back of the ambulance, applied a pressure dressing to Stacey's head, and then they were off, bumping over the potholes in the old castle lane before they reached the main road that would take them to the hospital.

Stacey spent as much of that time as she could smiling and laughing and joking with Jack, so that he would know that she was just fine, and when they wheeled her into A&E she loved how Jack held Daniel's hand—perhaps in lieu of not having Grover to hold.

They stood back, whilst a doctor examined her.

'It's an easy enough wound to fix. We'll clean it out and stitch it up for you—no problem. What caused the accident?'

Stacey explained.

'And you weren't feeling dizzy or anything before the fall? You just tripped?'

'That's right. I was tired from the uphill walk, but not dizzy.'

'Well, that seems straightforward. We might do an X-ray...just to confirm everything's okay. You've got quite a lump forming.'

Stacey winced. 'Great. Thanks.'

'An X-ray will mean radiation, so...any chance you could be pregnant?'

She blinked and looked at Jack and Daniel.

Daniel smiled. 'I'll take this one to get a drink. Come on, squirt.' And he led Jack away.

'I don't think so,' she told the doctor. 'I mean... I'm on the pill. But...' She frowned.

'But?' said the male doctor, smiling at her.

'But there was an incident when I missed a couple of pills. I started taking them again straight away, and I'm sure it's nothing, but I guess I ought to mention it.'

The doctor smiled. 'We'll do a pregnancy test, then—just to be on the safe side.'

She nodded, reassured. 'Okay.'

She didn't really think she would be. What were the chances? But a niggling voice at the back of her head told her that there was a chance, and she'd been right to mention it to the doctor. What must Daniel be thinking? Would he have seen that she thought it could be a possibility?

She hoped that he'd only thought she wanted him to take Jack away so that he wouldn't hear a conversation about her being on the pill. Little boys didn't need to know that kind of thing about their mothers—especially one who had just learned that his mother had a boyfriend now.

Poor Jack! He'd gone through so many changes and challenges recently and she really felt for him—even if he did seem to be taking everything in his stride. His confidence had soared since he'd come to live in Greenbeck, and she was so proud of him.

Just thinking about Jack made her feel as if she might cry, and she sniffed and wiped at her eyes just as the doctor came back and asked her if she would produce a urine sample for the test.

'Sure. No problem.'

She peed into a small bottle and returned to her cubicle, giving the sample to a nurse and settling back on the bed. For a moment she just lay there, trying to be conscious of relaxing. Lowering her shoulders. Not frowning. Loosening her jaw as if she was trying to get into a meditative state. And then she closed her eyes. For just a moment...

She was woken by the sound of the curtain being pulled back and she blinked awake to see Daniel at the side of her bed, with a sleeping Jack on his lap.

'How long have I been out?'

'About twenty minutes,' said Daniel quietly, and they both looked at the doctor who'd just come in.

'Dr Emery?' The doctor looked at Daniel. 'This is your husband?'

'No, we're not married.' She blushed.

'Would you prefer me to give you the results on your own, or…?'

She stared at the doctor. What was going on?

'No, we're both doctors. You can tell me in front of him.'

'You're sure?'

She nodded.

'The test shows that you're pregnant, Dr Emery. The levels of HCG in your blood indicate that you're in your first trimester.'

Stacey stared at the doctor who had just delivered the news, not quite believing what she was hearing. She glanced at Daniel, but he looked just as much in shock as she was!

'What? Could there be a mistake?'

'Of course there's always that possibility, but in my experience, no. We can take a blood sample to confirm, but I think we can probably accept the facts in this case. You say you're on the pill?'

She nodded. 'But I missed a couple…' she

said numbly, the news sinking in, her head wound forgotten.

Pregnant! A baby!

'How have you been feeling lately?'

Her brain felt slow. Murky. But the doctor's question made her think back over the last few days and weeks and she remembered the tiredness, and the headaches, and feeling hungry all the time. She'd felt sick on occasion. And now that she thought about it a bit more she had felt some tenderness in her breasts, but had put it down to the new bra she'd been wearing. She'd kept fiddling with the straps to get the fit right as it had seemed a little small.

I blamed the manufacturer!

'What about the X-ray?' she asked, her mind fixing on the one thing she could deal with right now.

'Well, there is a small risk to the foetus from radiation. We could cover you with a protective apron, or you could decide not to have an X-ray and we could monitor you for a while, to make sure you're okay. On palpation no fractures were indicated, but due to the swelling it might be advisory to have the X-ray. It is, of course, up to you. I'll leave you for a moment to decide.'

And then the doctor was gone again, swishing the curtain closed behind him.

Stacey looked down at Jack. He was going to be a big brother!

CHAPTER NINE

'YOU MISSED A couple of pills?' Daniel asked, in shock.

'It was before we... I noticed after... I...' her voice trailed off.

Clearly she was just as much in shock as he was!

On his lap, Jack continued to sleep, completely unaware of the tension in the cubicle.

'Why didn't you get the morning-after pill?'

She looked at him. Suddenly defensive. 'I couldn't! I'm allergic to it!'

Stacey was pregnant. With his baby!

He couldn't compute this! It was so unexpected! So out of left field! He wanted to get up and pace, move about, go and get some fresh air. But he couldn't, because he held her sleeping son on his lap.

He'd practically become a father to the little boy. And he'd been enjoying it. Selfishly spending as much time with Jack as he could because it fed a need he had inside himself and it had felt safe to do so. He wasn't his own flesh and blood. He'd figured that he'd feel somehow removed from him if anything happened. But now he was going to be an actual father to his own actual child…

He felt guilt drowning him in wave after wave of recrimination. They should have been more careful. He should have checked with her afterwards, when they'd had that talk about contraception and other partners they'd been with. He should have been clearer!

I can't deal with this.

Without thinking, just reacting, he gently scooped Jack up and lay him down on the bed next to Stacey.

'Where are you going?' she asked. 'We need to talk about this.'

'I can't! I just… I'm not leaving. I just… need to think about this.'

And he left the cubicle, walked away, needing space, needing some time to wrap his head around the enormous news that had just descended and changed his entire world in a single second.

'Daniel!'

He heard the pain in her voice. Heard the fear. And if this had been any other time he would have gone to her. Taken her hand. Asked her if she was all right.

But it wasn't any other time. Things had changed and he needed some time alone to process. He told himself that she must need it too. He'd told her he wasn't leaving her. He wasn't abandoning her the way that jerk Jerry had. He just needed a moment.

They both needed some space.

Stacey stared after him, hoping he'd been honest with her and would come back. Miserable, with tears beginning to fall, she picked up her mobile phone and called her gran.

'Hello?'

'Gran, it's me.'

'Darling, whatever's the matter? Why are you crying?'

'I'm in the hospital.'

'The hospital! Are you all right? Is it Jack?'

'No. No, it's not Jack. I had a fall. Hit my head. I'm okay, but... Could you come?'

'Of course, darling. We're on our way. Who has Jack?'

'I do. He's here with me. Asleep. I need you to come and take him.'

'Fifteen minutes, darling, and we'll be there—okay?'

She nodded and ended the call, dropping her phone back onto the bed and snuggling into Jack for comfort.

Daniel had left. *Left!* In the one moment when she needed him the most. When she herself was reeling from the news that she was pregnant with his child.

Pregnant.

This was monumental. She'd never expected this. Yes, she'd missed a couple of pills, but...

She groaned and squeezed Jack tightly.

The last time she'd been in this situation it hadn't gone well. Jerry had very quickly deserted her—told her that being a father was not something he felt able to do. That he had a hard enough time looking after himself and had no time in his life to look after a baby. And then he'd offered to pay for an abortion. Was Daniel going to do the same? She couldn't face such desertion again. Would he do something like that to her? He knew what had happened to her in the past—surely he wouldn't be the same? He was different. Daniel was a much better man. Wasn't he?

Having her own child had meant the world to her. Especially having lost her parents! Yes, she'd had her grandparents, but they'd been miles away and she had been alone, craving love. There'd been no way she'd get rid of her baby back then.

And now?

Daniel had disappeared. For good? Who knew?

Knowing of his past, and what had happened to Mason and Penny, she had no idea what was going through his head right now. Was he panicking? Was he terrified? Confused? Because if he was, then he could join the club! What did he think *she* was feeling? She hadn't planned this. She hadn't wanted another baby and set out to trap him, for crying out loud. This was a surprise to her, too!

When her grandparents arrived Daniel had still not returned. She told herself that he probably wouldn't now. She was trying to put on a brave face. Accept her fate. Accept that the same thing was happening again and she'd coped before and would do so again.

Her gran and grandad rushed into her cubicle, gasping when they saw her bandaged head and swollen face.

'Oh, my goodness!' Gran embraced her tightly, squeezing her, then pulling away. 'What happened?'

'I tripped on a rock. Up at the castle.'

'The castle?' said her grandad. 'What were you doing up there?'

'We went for a walk with Daniel.'

Her grandad looked around them. 'And where is he?'

She swallowed, feeling sad, but determined not to cry. 'He's gone.'

'Gone? I don't get it…' he said.

Her eyes welled with tears and she looked up at her gran, in the hope that she would find understanding.

She did.

Her gran took her hand. 'Will, why don't you take Jack out to the car and get him settled? I'll be there in a few minutes, okay?'

Her grandad nodded and gently woke Jack.

Jack kissed his mummy's bandage and smiled, then placed his hand in his great-grandad's and went with him.

When the boys were gone, her gran turned back to her and raised an eyebrow. 'What's going on?'

Stacey sucked in a breath. 'I'm pregnant.'

Genevieve Clancy gasped, but quickly controlled herself, clearly realising that now was not the time for dramatics. 'Daniel's baby?'

Stacey nodded.

'And he's not taken it very well?'

'No.'

'I can imagine… Where is he?'

'I don't know. He said he needed a moment to think, but that was ages ago. I think… I think the same thing is going to happen, Gran. I'm going to be on my own.'

'Hush, now. I don't believe that for a minute. Daniel is *not* Jerry. He's better than that. The two of you just need to talk. Sort things out. That's all. You've both had a shock.'

'You think he might come back?' she asked, hope filling her voice.

Gran smiled. 'I know he will. I know that

man and he loves you—whether he realises it yet or not. You mark my words. He'll be back.'

Stacey tried to smile through her tears, but it was hard.

She wanted to believe that Daniel loved her. She really did. Because if he did it would solve everything.

But her hopes continued to fade with every second that her cubicle remained empty of him.

Daniel sat with his head in his hands in a small garden in the hospital grounds. It wasn't a huge garden. Just a circle lined with benches, a few shrubs, a couple of ornamental roses and in the centre a dwarf willow tree.

At the base of the tree was a small plaque.

This garden was built in memory of
Nurse Wendy Sinclair,
who served forty-two years
here on the renal ward.
It is in recognition of her
service and the care that
all our nurses provide to every
patient who walks through our doors.

*Wendy knew the importance of
having a space
to think and relax,
and it is our hope that this garden
provides a comfort and a haven
to all who need it.*

Well, he needed it. Space. Comfort. A place to think.

He'd not been able to think in that small cubicle. Not with the doctor there. Not with Jack on his lap—a big reminder that he was already in much too deep with Stacey and her family. And not after hearing the news that he'd got Stacey pregnant and was going to be a father again.

He'd accepted that his family had died with Penny and Mason, and he'd never, ever considered starting another with another woman. Maybe for a time there he'd allowed himself to play at being part of a family, and the time he'd spent with Stacey and Jack had been amazing. And not just with Stacey and Jack, but Genevieve and William. They had all embraced him wholeheartedly.

What was he doing? He'd run. He'd escaped

when suddenly it had all got very real. He couldn't imagine what Stacey was feeling. Hadn't her last partner deserted her on finding out she was pregnant?

I haven't deserted her. I just need space.

Could he do it again?

I have no choice. It's already happened. That baby exists.

The question was, was he strong enough to be vulnerable again? Just seeing Stacey fall and bang her head had scared him. All that blood! When he'd been trapped in that car in Hawaii with Penny and Mason, the blood had dripped down Penny's face too, and seeing Stacey like that had catapulted him back in time, filling him with the sensation that he was helpless and useless and the whole world was going to implode.

I thought that I was going to lose her.

The waiting for the ambulance had been terrible. He'd sat there, dabbing at her head, checking her vitals, thinking that with every minute they were waiting a big haematoma could be forming. At any second she would pass out, or start to seize, and there'd be no help for her. He'd be alone again. Helpless.

It had all been too much.

But the head wound had been the least of it! He was going to be a father again, and in Stacey's womb the baby they had made was already growing. It was innocent. This new life that they had created!

Am I strong enough to lay my heart on the line again? What if something happens to the baby? To Stacey? To Jack? What if I can't protect them?

He stared at Wendy Sinclair's plaque, reading the words over and over again. She'd been a nurse. He was a doctor. Same as Stacey. They all cared. That was what they did. They cared and they tried to make people better, sometimes despite the odds, and they would continue to fight for their patients.

If he could do it for them, surely he could do it for his own family?

The idea of walking away was impossible. He knew that deep inside. Being a father was the most wonderful thing a man could do. Being present, raising a child, was a gift. One that he would never ignore. Nor would he want to.

Daniel got to his feet and turned to look at the hospital.

He'd been gone long enough.

CHAPTER TEN

'HERE'S A LEAFLET on head wounds and what to look out for,' said the doctor. 'Rest easy for a couple of days, and in about ten days you can get those stitches removed by your GP.'

Stacey nodded, accepting the leaflet, smiling, trying to be brave. Gran had gone with Jack and Grandad to take Jack home to bed. Gran had told her they would stay, so they could take her home, too, but Stacey had wanted to be alone for a while and Jack needed his sleep. Nor did she need her gran and grandad hanging around the hospital. She knew it gave them bad memories they didn't want to experience all over again.

'Thank you,' she said now.

'You're welcome. Take care—and watch your step from now on.'

She smiled. 'I will.'

When the doctor had left Stacey stood up, sliding her mobile back into her pocket. She looked up when the curtain swished open again, expecting a nurse.

Only it wasn't.

It was Daniel.

Her heart thudded in her chest and she felt herself grow hot, her cheeks flushing. The need to cry again was so strong she had to dab at her eyes.

'If you're coming back to tell me it's all over, there's no need.'

'That's not what I've come to tell you,' he said, stepping forward.

And that was when she realised he was holding a carrier bag. She looked up into his eyes in question.

'This is for you.' He passed her the bag.

Frowning, confused, she opened it and looked inside, gasping as she saw a little white baby onesie. It was tiny. Newborn to three months—that was the sizing. Pure white, with an embroidered teddy on the front.

'I got something unisex…seeing as we don't know what it is yet.'

The onesie was so cute she wanted to cry, but still she held back her tears. 'I don't understand.'

He stepped forward, took her hand in his. 'I needed a moment.' He smiled ruefully. 'It took longer than I expected.'

'A moment for what?'

'To realise what I have. What a gift you are. You. Jack.' He looked down at her belly. 'The baby.'

Stacey sniffed, looking into his eyes with love. She couldn't help herself. 'Tell me more.'

'I panicked. I thought that I wouldn't be able to protect you. I failed before, and I knew I couldn't feel like that again. But then I realised, sitting out there, that I most certainly couldn't protect you if I wasn't around. If I was at a distance. Hiding. Thinking I was doing the right thing for me. But it's not just about me. And I promise you that I will not panic any more. I will not leave you. Any of you. You've brought so much to my life in these last few weeks and I can't imagine you not being there. I need you. *All* of you. If you'll have me.'

He reached up to stroke her face, wiped her tears away with his thumb, smiling at her with such love.

She hiccupped a laugh. Gave a smile. 'I'm

scared, Daniel. Scared of what all this means. The changes that are about to happen. I never planned this. Never expected it. But… I know I can do it. I'm strong enough. And what makes me happy is having you by my side.' She laughed. 'I knew you were trouble the moment I laid eyes on you! But you're the best kind of trouble. The only kind of trouble.'

She leaned forward. Dropped a kiss onto his lips.

'I love you. And Jack does, too. We can do this, you and I. We can do anything together.'

He smiled and nodded. 'We can. I love you, too.'

And they kissed.

There was a huge turn-out for the fete. The whole village had shown up, and as an added bonus the sun was shining, making everyone doubly happy. There were food stands filling the air with the aroma of hot dogs and burgers and candy floss, a doughnut van and a juice bar. There were clowns and jugglers—even one who was walking around on stilts!

Stacey could hear a voice speaking through

a megaphone. She couldn't make out the words, but she felt she knew the voice. Was it Zach? No. It couldn't be. What would he be doing on a megaphone?

Everywhere she looked she saw smiling faces. People were looking as happy as she felt.

Walking hand in hand with Daniel, she leaned in and whispered to him, 'You're sure I look okay?'

She touched her fingertips to where she'd hit her head a couple of weeks ago. The stitches were out, and the swelling was down, but there was still some lingering green-yellow bruising, and she'd looked in the mirror that morning to hide it with make-up.

'You're the most beautiful woman here.' He smiled and planted a brief kiss on her lips as Jack ran on ahead to try his luck at the football game.

They passed the cake marquee and Stacey waved at her gran and grandad, who were inside. Her gran was fussing over a three-dimensional cake that she'd made to look like a lighthouse. It looked amazing, and she hoped that Gran would win. Next to the cake stand was the vegetable stall, and she peered inside to see if she could see her grandfather's cabbage and the marrow that he'd entered. But there were so many items of a giant nature it was hard to know which were his.

Their destination was the baby cosplay marquee. They were due to judge there, along with Zach, and they could already see him standing there, holding on to a clipboard. Beside him stood Hannah, their advanced nurse practitioner, who was all smiles and playing with her necklace.

'How are those two getting along?' Stacey asked Daniel.

'I don't know,' Daniel replied. 'But they look good right now, don't you think?'

Stacey nodded. 'You should ask Zach.'

'I will. Later.'

At that moment they reached the marquee and there were a lot of hellos. Zach clapped Daniel on the back and then leaned forward to kiss Stacey on the cheek. They both smiled at Hannah.

'Ready to judge?' Zach asked.

'Not really.'

Zach grinned and nodded towards Stacey's

belly. 'Just think. Next year, you can enter *your* little one!'

Stacey cradled her belly protectively. 'Er... we'll think about it!' she said, and laughed.

Walter came up to them and gave her and Daniel a clipboard each. Each entrant had their name, age and character written down, and a space for them to enter a mark out of ten. Inside the marquee they saw lots of frantic parents trying to present their babies. Some were blissfully asleep in their costumes, others were crying, whilst some just looked bemused.

'Off you go,' said Walter. 'You give each entrant a mark out of ten and at the end we'll tally the scores. In the case of a draw, it's down to the head judge to decide on the winner—that's you, Dr Fletcher.'

Zach nodded and let go of Hannah's hand.

Stacey and Daniel followed them into the marquee and began judging. There were lots of amazing costumes. Dragons, a mermaid, Robin Hood... Their eyes were assaulted by such a wide breadth of imagination.

Stacey looked at all the babies, wanting to give them all ten out of ten, but she knew she couldn't, so tried to be as fair as she could. She spoke to each parent, and each child if it was awake, and when she was done headed into the judges' tent to tally up the scores and hand their marking sheets to Walter, who would officiate.

'I'm so nervous!' Stacey said. 'And hungry!'

'Want me to fetch you something?' asked Daniel.

'No, I'm fine. I can wait.'

'Nonsense. I'll get you something.'

Daniel had headed off in an instant.

Zach turned to her. 'You've made him a very happy man again, you know. It's good to see him like this.'

'Well, he's made me very happy, too,' Stacey replied, smiling. 'Ecstatic, even. And Jack adores Daniel. I could never have hoped for this much happiness when I came back to Greenbeck. I'd hoped for *some*, but all of this… It's magical.'

Daniel returned with a glazed doughnut. Her favourite. He kissed her on the lips after he'd passed it to her.

'I'll be huge at this rate!' She laughed, biting into the doughnut.

The prize for the best costume went to a one-year-old dressed up as a spider, and now their judging duties were done she and Daniel headed away from the village green over to the Wishing Bridge. On the way Daniel waved to Jack and gave him a nod, and her son joined them.

Standing there, arm in arm, they looked down at the water beneath them for a brief moment, and then Daniel was turning her to face him, smiling, looking deeply into her eyes.

'I have something to ask you.'

'Oh?' Stacey glanced at Jack, who was grinning broadly.

Daniel looked nervous suddenly. And then he got down on one knee.

She gasped, stepping back, looking at the two people she loved most in the world.

Daniel nodded at Jack, smiled, and then reached into his pocket and produced a small box.

'I've already asked Jack for his permission.

He gave it. But I need to ask *you*, Stacey Emery, love of my life, if you will marry me?'

He opened the small box and inside was a gorgeous diamond and sapphire ring.

She almost couldn't believe it! He'd proposed!

'Yes! Yes! Oh, my God, yes!'

Daniel got to his feet and slipped the ring onto her finger, and then he was kissing her, and she was laughing and crying, and Jack was hugging them both. Daniel lifted Jack up and they all held one another, and loved one another, and Stacey knew without a shadow of a doubt that she would never be alone ever again. That she had found her happiness here in Greenbeck. That Daniel would be there for them all.

She was loved. Protected. Adored.

Taking a step back into her past had propelled her into a wonderful future.

She kissed her son, then she kissed Daniel, and with a hand on her belly she knew that wishes did come true.

* * * * *

LET'S TALK

Romance

For exclusive extracts, competitions
and special offers, find us online:

f facebook.com/millsandboon

◎ @millsandboonuk

🐦 @millsandboon

Or get in touch on 0844 844 1351*

For all the latest titles coming soon,
visit millsandboon.co.uk/nextmonth

*Calls cost 7p per minute plus your phone company's price per
minute access charge

Want even more
ROMANCE?

Join our bookclub today!

**Visit millsandbook.co.uk/Bookclub
and save on brand new books.**

MILLS & BOON